1 MONTH OF
FREE
READING

at

www.ForgottenBooks.com

By purchasing this book you are eligible for one month membership to ForgottenBooks.com, giving you unlimited access to our entire collection of over 1,000,000 titles via our web site and mobile apps.

To claim your free month visit:

www.forgottenbooks.com/free805824

ISBN 978-0-267-00331-0
PIBN 10805824

THE RAPIN

BY

HENRY DE VERE STACPOOLE

AUTHOR OF "PIERROT"

NEW YORK

HENRY HOLT AND COMPANY

1899

THE MERSHON COMPANY PRESS,
RAHWAY, N. J.

FOREWORD.

IN the rooms of my friend Otto Struve there hangs a parrot cage containing a somewhat dejected-looking lark. It was given to him by Gustave Garnier, the man who took the Prix de Rome last year—or was it the year before?—and whose picture of a girl was bought by the state for I do not know how many thousand francs before it had hung a fortnight in the Salon. A story connects the painter and the picture and the bird—a story whose name ought to have been " Célestin " but for that eternal unfitness of things which makes the comedy of real life an inverted image of the comedy of romance and demands for the story of Célestin the title of " Toto," or, if it please you better, " The Rapin."

H. de V. S.

CONTENTS.

Contents.

PART IV.

THE RAPIN.

Part 1

CHAPTER I.

TOTO.

THE room was filled with an odor of Nice violets, fur, and the faint scent of caravan tea. A number of candles burning under rose-colored shades lit the place subduedly, whilst through the great windows the broad white expanse of the Boulevard Haussmann reflected the cold light of the April evening with a suggestion of snow.

The Princesse de Cammora's "Five-o'clock" was exhausting itself, Madeline Frémont of the Comédie Française having just departed, also the Duchesse M—— de M——, the wheels of whose barouche had a moment ago rumbled away round the corner of the Rue de Courcelles.

The Rapin.

Nothing was left now but for the remaining few to take their departure. There was nothing to keep them, yet they clung after the fashion of grounds to the bottom of a coffee-cup.

There were three ancient dames and an old Marquis, all relics of the Empire, all boring each other to death, and lingering on in the dim hope of being asked to dinner. A pretty girl in furs and picture hat stood at one of the windows, her furs thrown open, and her eyes fixed meditatively upon the street. M. le Marquis Sobrahon de Nani was explaining to two old Empire women the difference between the Comédie Française now and " then," whilst the Princesse de Cammora sat near the tea-table with its little cups and dishes of *petits fours* and what-nots, conversing volubly with another Princesse, painted, after the fashion of her hostess, with the roses of eighteen on the parchment of fifty.

" I should never have called him Toto," wailed the Princesse de Cammora, whilst the girl at the window pricked her ears beneath her picture hat, and seemed more than ever

absorbed by the Boulevard Haussmann. " It
was the wretched *Nounou's* fault; she came
from Tarbes. Really, if I had known the
worry of nurses, I would never have had a child.
She stole everything she could lay her hands upon
—my bracelets, my rings, the drops off the grand
chandelier; everything was found in her box; it was
like the nest of a magpie. She spoke as if she held
pins in her mouth, and she could never pronounce
the name Désiré, so she called him Toto. Her
husband was an Italian from Ventimiglia, and he
was called Toto, and so it pleased the good God
that my child should receive this outrageous nick-
name. Everyone calls him Toto now, and the
wretched boy, when I accuse him of his wildnesses,
throws the name in my teeth, and asks me how he
can live seriously with such a pug-dog name attached to him. I assure you, my dear Mathilde,
the amounts I have paid during the last month
would horrify you—*bills* that he has run up! Oh,
no, never give a child a thoughtless name! I assure you, in this world *things often begin in jest
which end very much in earnest.* If you could only

guess one-half of this mad boy's wickedness and absurd "—here the other Princesse made a grimace at Helen Powers, the American millionairess in the picture hat, as if to say, " She is listening "—" and absurd good-nature! " resumed the mother of Toto, snapping her scent-bottle lid—" wickednesses without a particle of real wickedness in them, but none the less annoying to a mother for that. Only the other night he came home without any money. It seems he had met a poor old woman near the Madeleine, and for a freak upset the basket of apples she was carrying; then, to pay her for her apples, what must he do but empty all the money in his pocket—some seventeen napoleons, as I afterwards learnt—into her lap! That is the sort of wickedness my Toto indulges in."

" Ah! " moaned the other, shaking a crumb off her muff, " such wickednesses are enough to open the gates of heaven. And this poor old woman? "

" She has retired into the country to live on this bounty. Toto, I believe, went to-day to see her and carry her some more assistance. *Mon Dieu!* "

Someone who had slipped into the room, and

who had been standing unobserved behind the heavy curtains of the door listening to the lies in the air, slipped out now like a hound freed from the leash, and embraced the Princesse de Cammora, nearly dislocating her neck, and brushing the bloom off her right cheek. It was Toto.

Never was created a more debonair or devil-may-care-looking person than Toto; the name fitted him like a glove, at least now, as he stood helping himself to sweets from the table and laughing at his mother. He looked about eighteen; his real age, however, was twenty-two, and he possessed that brightness of eye and vivacity of manner which sometimes indicates genius, and sometimes excellent health, combined with a highly strung nervous temperament. Affecting Longchamps and art, the society of pugilists and men of letters, shining here as a *flâneur*, there as the patron of little poets, and lately—somewhat in secret—as a painter of pictures painted all by himself, he presented a queer variety of that always amusing insect, the " child of the age."

" Where the devil can Toto have come from? "

asked Otto Struve, the art critic, one day, tilting his hat back in momentary astonishment. " His father, on his own showing, was a miser; his mother never laughed. They marry, and live for ten years unproductive as a pair of icebergs, and then produce Toto, who only stops smiling when he laughs or yawns, and spending money when he sleeps; whose head produces the most extraordinary ideas in Paris; whom God constructed with one eye on the gingerbread fair, and whom the devil made a prince of—a prince of twenty, with the ideas of ten and the vices of sixty! "

" I am a changeling," had replied Toto, bonneting Otto Struve's hat in such a manner that it had to be cut off with scissors.

Now he saluted everyone at once—Helen Powers, and his mother, and the old Princesse de Harnac. The Empire decadents came out of their corner like lizards towards sunshine, and he promptly invited them to stay to dinner, knowing that his mother hated them, and that he would be dining out himself.

" I have been to a cock-fight at Chantilly," he

explained, glancing down at the suit of tweed in which he was dressed. "The police broke it up, and we had to run; but they wired, and the police stopped me at the Nord. They let me go when I gave my address; then I took a cab from the Nord, and coming downhill we ran over a dog—nothing but accidents."

The old Marquis de Nani lifted up his hands in pretended horror to please his hostess, and lowered them again and took a pinch of snuff when that lady frowned slightly.

"I do not see any particular harm in cock-fighting," said Toto's mother, appealing to the company generally, and Helen Powers in particular. "I know it sounds cruel, but, then, they say the cocks enjoy it."

"That must be so," said the Marquis, replacing his snuff-box in his pocket, "or else they would not fight."

"But——" said Miss Powers, and stopped. Her eyes had met Toto's eyes. He was standing almost behind his mother and making grimaces, as if to say, "For goodness' sake don't begin an argument, or we shall never get away." " But," said Miss Powers, shamelessly turning the conversation in the wished-for direction, " you promised me, M. le Prince, to show me those pictures on which you were engaged."

" That is why I came back in such a hurry," replied Toto. " And if you will accompany me now to my studio, come on, and M. le Marquis also, for he is a connoisseur. No one else; my bashfulness will not hold more than two comfortably."

He led the way, laughing, out of the room and up the great staircase, Helen Powers following and the old Marquis de Nani toiling after, his Empire legs unaccustomed to such unstately swiftness. On the top landing Prince Toto opened a door and switched on the electric light, exposing to view a large square studio.

One could see at a glance that this was the atelier of no dilettante. Work was written on the place from the top light to the boarded floor. Several massive easels stood about with the air of willing laborers awaiting their jobs; there was a throne and some drapery; a painting-jacket hung suspended from a nail in the wall, along which a number of canvases stood with their backs to the room like children undergoing punishment.

Helen Powers felt utterly astonished. She had known Toto some time, and she liked him more, perhaps, than she had ever liked another man; but she was alive to his faults, his irresponsibility, his childish wildnesses. Here, then, was a revelation of honest hard work more amazing than a jewel in a toad's head.

"I know the place is rather bare," said Toto apologetically, "but it's good enough to work in. It's a bit cold now, but I light a fire when I am working at the nude, and then it is like a furnace. Here's a thing."

He took one of the canvases in Coventry and placed it upon an easel.

"Oh, my God, how beautiful!" said the old Marquis de Nani, putting on his pince-nez as the electric light fell full upon the indifferent-looking daub exposed so ruthlessly to view.

"Everyone says that," said Toto, so innocently

and so frankly that the tears almost rose to Helen Powers' eyes.

"I have never seen a picture quite like that," continued the Marquis. "There is an air about it, a something indefinable about it. Those bulrushes"—it was a naked nymph trying to screen herself behind bulrushes—"those bulrushes seem to quiver in the wind."

"Otto Struve said Ingres might have painted it," said Toto, with a smile that made him look like an angel by Raphael. He had several smiles at his command, and most of them made him look like a good-humored devil. "But they turned it away from the Salon, though I'd had half of the hanging committee to dinner the night before and made them jolly. Otto said the other half were jealous. I'll have the whole lot next time if I can get them. Here's a John the Baptist. What do you think of that?"

John the Baptist was brought forth, and a Sisera and Jael, all treated in the old original manner, with a difference due to want of skill. A lamentable Holofernes appeared and vanished.

" Those are all classical," said the author after De Nani had almost bleated himself hoarse in their praise, revolving in his own mind the while a project which had for aim the borrowing of five hundred francs from this illustrious artist. " But this is original, or, at least, I think so."

He exposed a blind beggar and his daughter, filled with a mawkish sentimentality strangely at variance with the known character of the Prince.

Helen Powers looked on. Her liking for Toto had rapidly altered. This art show had supplied the crystallizing thread for her feelings to seize upon. She was now mournfully in love with him. It was as if he had suddenly become maimed and needful of her pity. Her mind became filled with anger against Otto Struve and old De Nani and all the other sycophants or sneerers who had belauded this poor boy and his works. She felt a kindness for cock-fighting as she gazed upon the blind beggar and his whining yellow-ocher daughter, a strange emotion in the breast of a delicately nurtured girl, and, so to speak, one of the minor miracles wrought by art.

Toto, as anxious for praise as a baby for milk, looked at her with dark expectant eyes.

"I don't know what to say," said the poor girl. "I know nothing about art, but I think I like Jael the best; but don't take my opinion, please, for I am an utter ignoramus. What a time it must have taken you to paint all these!"

"That's just what it didn't," replied the artist joyously, as if he had outwitted art by some clever trick. "I paint like lightning. You see, I haven't much time to spare; but I love it, and give all the time I can. I have often thought of throwing everything else over and giving all my time to art."

"Oh, do!" said Helen earnestly.

"Do what?" asked the lightning artist.

"Give up all your time to it, be in earnest over it. Nothing is done in this world without earnestness of purpose. I am sure you would be—would be—a great artist if you worked. Give up cock-fighting and all that, and take seriously to art."

"Do you know," said Prince Toto, putting the

blind beggar away, "I have often thought of kicking the world over. I've seen everything and done everything worth doing, and I feel as old as the hills."

"He, he, he!" bleated the Marquis de Nani.

"Then why not begin at once?" said Helen. "If you are only in earnest and have purpose, you will succeed, for I am sure you have genius."

The unlucky little word had escaped unweighed by the speaker. Toto nodded reflectively, as if to some thought that had just left the shelter of his curly head to take visible form.

"I am sure that M. le Prince has more genius in that head of his than resides in all those palette-scrapers one sees in the Louvre," declared the Marquis de Nani, taking a pinch of snuff and making a little old-fashioned bow, as if to the observation that had just escaped from him. He held out his box, and the amateur genius took a pinch and sneezed frightfully.

"And genius," continued the old gentleman reflectively, adding on two hundred and fifty francs to the intended loan, "it seems to me, never has a more charming home than with a man of birth; birth comes out even in a picture. That blind beggar and his little daughter. Ah, my God! cannot one see the sympathy of the well-born for the poor illuminating it? I never praise—old age has made a wreck of my enthusiasm; but my heart rekindles when I see art thus wrested from the hands of the hateful *canaille* by one of *us*."

"Indeed!" said Helen Powers, whose father had been a pig-slaughterer.

"Indeed yes, mademoiselle!" replied the old man, winking and blinking like a delirious goat, whilst Toto looked on with a grin. "I have left all my ambition behind me, buried beneath the ruins of the Empire, else would I wish to be young like M. le Prince, and gifted like the painter of these treasures."

"Now I must be going," said Helen Powers.

"And I," said Toto; "I have a dinner on at the Grand Café."

"Why," cried the Marquis, seeing his seven hundred and fifty francs vanishing, "I thought you were going to dine here, at home!"

" Not I indeed! " said Toto; " I am giving a little dinner of my own."

" Alas! " moaned the old man, " I had counted upon your pleasant company. I am desolated."

" Well, bring your desolation to my feast."

" But——" said M. le Marquis, glancing down at his frock-coat.

" Oh, that's nothing," replied Toto; " I am going to dine in these."

" Then," said the other, " I will go down and make my excuses to the Princesse. Pardon me, mademoiselle."

" With pleasure," answered Helen Powers, and he tripped away like a boy.

" Toto," said the girl,—she called him Toto sometimes when no one was by,—" beware of that old man and all these people who praise you; there's nothing so bad for an artist as praise. Art," she continued, gazing at him and speaking as if she knew all about it, " is always capable of improvement. I mean the artist is. Don't mind what he says about the *canaille*—remember Millet;

go and get a blouse like a common man, work like a common man. All people are common in art till they have made princes of themselves like Raphael and Michael Angelo."

" That is what I have been thinking lately," said the unhappy Toto, imbibing this lesson greedily because it fitted in with his whim, and whims with Toto sometimes lasted for months—Mlle. Dumaresque lasted for three, and cost him sixty thousand francs. " Just what I have been thinking: what is the use of all this life? I'm sick of it. If one could invent a new way of spending money or something new to eat—but it's just the same old round. I've thought of committing suicide, sometimes."

" Oh, don't, Toto—don't speak like that! "

" I won't; besides, I didn't think of it seriously."

" Tell me, Toto," said Helen, in the voice of a mother speaking to a child, " do you ever think seriously of anything? "

" I think I do," said Toto, rubbing his cheek against a corner of her sealskin jacket, because it was soft and gratified his sensual nature. " I have thought seriously of running away from here, and living by my painting—seriously."

A look came into his face that astonished her, a look of iron determination or leaden obstinacy, she could not tell which; but it made her feel sure that if he ever did commit such a folly he would adhere to it till he was famous or, a more probable eventuality, dead.

" For," said Toto, " I have got a queer sort of feeling lately: it's money-hate. It's awfully funny, for it's not exactly money-hate, but it's a want to make money and not spend it. It's like a man that wants to dig."

Helen looked at him proudly.

" Here," thought she, " is the *man* breaking out; the boy is dying away. Toto will be a great man yet." Alas for Helen's thoughts! What woman can ever understand a man? what woman could ever have understood Toto? Otto Struve alone got him in a true focus, but of that anon.

" Besides," said Toto, still rubbing his cheek softly against the fur, a caress which Helen took to herself, " I feel that I—I want to protect someone, to feed them and work for them, and I haven't anyone to—protect, for everyone I know is so rich."

Helen's eyes became dim. She was just about to say something hopeful in reply, when the old Marquis entered the room, jubilant like a school-boy going to a treat.

"Now good-by," said Helen, pressing Toto's hand. "No, don't come with me; I'll find my way. Good-by, M. le Marquis;" and she vanished to say good-by to her hostess and find her coachman, who for the last two hours had been outside shivering in the cold April evening.

As Toto and his companion passed the drawing-room door, the Princesse appeared for a moment and drew the old fellow aside.

"Be sure and take care of my boy, Marquis, and give him good advice."

"Princesse, be assured," replied the gentleman of the old school, placing his hand upon his heart, "*I* will give him good advice; and," he whispered, "it is all right in that quarter. She called him a genius, and that tickles a young man's vanity, and

I am almost sure kisses passed between them during my absence from the room. I am not a bad judge of these affairs, and I predict——"

He nodded mysteriously, and the Princesse de Cammora smiled under her paint and powder the smile of the happy mother.

CHAPTER II.

" TELL me, my dear boy," bleated old De Nani, who wanted to get the affair over and done with before dinner, " could you till the end of next month, when my rents from Normandy will be due —could you accommodate me with a little loan? "

" Yes, rather," said Toto. " How much? "

" Seven hundred and fifty francs would save me the necessity of approaching a money-lender," said the old fellow, trembling in his shoes at the amount for which he was asking. " But——"

Toto stopped under the lamp at the corner of the Rue de Courcelles where it cuts the Boulevard Haussmann. He took a note-case from his pocket.

" Here's a note for a thousand. You can let me have it some time. I haven't anything smaller."

" A million million thanks! " cried De Nani, grabbing the note and gritting his false teeth to

think that he might have asked for two thousand
and obtained it just as easily—"a million thanks!
Why, my dear boy, what a doleful yawn! One
might fancy you bored."

"I am, to death."

"May I make you a little prescription?" inquired the old man, in whom the prospect of the
coming dinner operated like an elixir of youth.

"A prescription for ennui? Yes."

"Get married."

"I have been thinking that myself."

"She is a very charming girl."

"Who?"

"Mlle.—what do you call her?—Powhair?"

"Bah!" said Toto. "I'd as soon think of marrying the Bank of France."

"*Parbleu!*" murmured De Nani. "What an
extraordinary remark! But everything that
comes from Prince Toto is extraordinary, even his
pictures."

He had the bank-note safe in his pocket, and
could allow himself the luxury of a little irony in
the guise of praise.

" Firstly," said Toto, " she's too rich; and secondly, my mother wants me to marry her."

" True," said De Nani. " She is also *gauche*, and speaks through her beautiful nose like a trumpet."

" She is good enough as a girl," said the Prince with a frightful yawn as they turned down the Rue Tronchet.

" Well, then," said De Nani, " try a mistress."

" I have four," replied Toto dolorously.

" Dismiss them."

" I have, but they cling on."

" Get drunk."

" Can't. I was born drunk, and am beginning to get sober. That is what's the matter with me, I think."

" Try opium."

" Makes me sick."

" Ether capsules."

" Worse."

" Go into the country and make love to a milk-maid."

" Never done that," said Toto reflectively.

" I did once when I was young. *Mon Dieu!* she followed me to Paris. No, I would advise you to leave that alone; nothing clings like a milkmaid. Try, try, try a glass of absinthe."

They stopped at a café and had a glass of absinthe, for which Toto paid.

" I would like to get drunk on absinthe and die in my cups," said De Nani, who was a man of original sins, frost-bound by poverty, but blossoming now under the warm influence of Toto.

" Let's," said the Prince, beginning to laugh.

" Now I have made you laugh!" cried the old fellow triumphantly. "And here we are at the Grand Café. No, my Toto, we will not die just yet, while there are Grand Cafés, and good dinners, and pretty girls adorning the world. Tu, tu, tu! how the lights flare!"

They entered, the old man following Toto and pursing out his hideous old lips. One could see his stomach working through his face as they passed first to the lavatory with the frescoed ceilings, where Toto washed himself vehemently with his coat off, and De Nani looked

on. Then, led by the assistant head-waiter, they
ascended to the private room where the Prince's
friends were waiting.

Three men only—Pelisson, of the *Journal des
Débats;* Gaillard, a mystical poet, pantheistic,
melancholic, with no very fixed belief in anything,
save, perhaps, the works of Gaillard; and Otto
Struve, the art critic.

Pelisson, a powerfully built fellow, singularly like
De Blowitz, even to the pointed whiskers, was of
the type of man who pushes the world aside with
his shoulders, whilst he pushes it forward with his
head.   Gaillard, who was remarkable for his high
collars, pointed beard, and the childish interest he
took in little things unconnected with his profound
art, sat astride a chair watching Pierre Pelisson
juggling with a wine-glass, a fish-knife, and a serviette.   By the fireplace stood Otto Struve, a man
with a hatchet-shaped face, who seemed in the last
stages of consumption, and weighed down by the
cares of the whole world, which he bore with sup-
pressed irritation.

Toto's entrance was the entrance of money.

Everyone forgot everyone else for a moment; the electric lamps seemed to blaze more brightly; waiters suddenly appeared, mutes shod with velvet and bearing the *hors d'œuvre*.

" M. le Marquis de Nani," said Toto, introducing his friend; and they took their seats.

Old De Nani ate his oysters, glancing sideways, this way and that way, at the triumvirate of talent, as if to say, " Who the devil are you? " and " Who the devil are you? " Pelisson groaned and grunted; he was writing the beginning of a leading article in that wonderful head of his, where a clerk always sat taking notes in indelible ink, an artist beside him taking sketch-portraits of everyone and pictures of everything. Toto looked bored and the dinner unpromising, till suddenly Struve broke the ice by choking over his soup. With the laughter, conversation broke out and babbled. The fish was served, and one might have fancied twenty people were talking, Toto's voice raised shrill against Gaillard's periods, and the trumpet tones of Pelisson dominating all like the notes of a sax-horn.

" I don't believe in God, you say? " said Gaillard, savagely attacking a fillet of sole. " Well, perhaps not, according to your ideas; according to mine, I have the pleasure of worshiping a god. He has fifty-three names. The Chinese call him Fot; benighted Asiatic tribes, Buddha; Kempfer, by the way, wrote it——"

" No, no, no! " cried Toto. " No theology, or I'll turn M. le Marquis de Nani upon you, and he'll eat you up, for he's an atheist."

" An atheist! " cried Pelisson, turning his broad face on De Nani. " I thought they were all dead. M. de Nani, beware! They'll kill you and stuff you for the Musée Carnavalet."

" I'll stuff him," shouted Toto, imagining himself a wit. " What shall it be, Marquis—bran, sawdust? "

" Ortolans," answered De Nani, too busily engaged in stuffing himself to find passage for more than one word.

" By my soul, the Marquis is right! " cried the great newspaper man. " An atheist stuffed with ortolans is all they want to complete their collec-

tion now they have crowned their idiocy by buying
——'s collection of bronzes."

" Talking of crowns," came the insidious lisp of
Struve, " have you heard the news? Willy Hohen-
zollern has—guess what."

" Written a farce? "

" Painted his face? "

" Become a telegraph clerk? "

" Gone mad," replied Struve.

" What's his madness? " roared Pelisson, glaring
at this opposition newsman.

" They say he fancies himself an Emperor."

" Throw flowers over him to cool him," cried
Toto, snatching a rose out of a dish and flinging it
in Struve's face as the *entrée* was brought in.

De Nani listened to the random conversation as
he ate, or at least seemed to; a dull flush was ap-
parent under the paint on his face. Each guest
had his own attendant, and the service was conducted with the precision of mechanism. The
glass of the Marquis was always full, yet he was
continually emptying it; like the old gentleman at
M. de Richelieu's feast, he felt his teeth growing

again, and for a little while, under the influence of the powerful Rhone wines, his youth seemed to return.

" Talking of art," said Gaillard, fingering the stem of his wineglass delicately and turning to Toto, " a rumor reached me to-day through De Brie, the editor of the *Boulevard*—you know De Brie? It was to the effect that our host——"

" Yes."

" That our host," continued Gaillard, turning to the others, " wearied by the incapacity of the two salons to appreciate genius——"

" To appreciate genius," echoed Struve.

" Is about to found an art school."

De Nani leaned back in his chair and slipped a button of his waistcoat, as if to give room for the sycophant to ramp.

" And who," said he, " would be fitter to found an art school than our host—ahu!—who, may I ask, M. Veillard? "

" Gaillard."

" Maillard—than our illustrious host, ahu! I

have seen his works, *ventre St. Gris!* Ahu! I am not a man of yesterday, M. Baillard; my memory carries me back to the time before women wore hoops."

" Indeed," murmured Struve, who had placed the rose flung at him by Toto with its stalk in his glass of champagne, and was staring at it with the rapt air of a poet.

" Indeed yes, monsieur, I was born on the edge of the First Empire. I saw the new Napoleon rise —you, sir, have only seen him vanish."

" I have seen many a napoleon vanish," mourned Struve; " but go on—your tale charms me. Pelisson, listen."

" Go to the devil!" said Pelisson, who was now writing with the speed of fire and a stylographic pen on a long strip of paper, using the table for a desk.

" I have seen the art galleries of Europe," continued De Nani, now three parts drunk, and unconscious that he was making a fool of himself before the first art critic in Europe, " and I unhesitatingly proclaim M. le Prince's work to be on a level—allowing of course for youth—on a level with the best I have seen."

"Oh, rot! oh, rubbish!" cried Toto, blushing furiously and flinging flowers at the great bent head of Pelisson, whilst that journalist, wallowing in his journalese, only grunted and growled in a far-away manner and wrote the more quickly. "*I* can't paint, *I* can't draw—might if I took to it really. Pelisson, you pig! wake up and eat your pudding."

"I have said what I have said," concluded De Nani, attacking his ice-pudding with all the youth-ful nonchalance of your man who wears false teeth.

"And my rose is drunk," said Struve, as the rose tumbled out of the glass.

"*I* can't paint," murmured Toto again with the air of a spoilt child.

"Toto!" demanded Struve, placing the rose lan-guidly in his coat, "how much wine have you drunk?"

"Why?"

"Because a lot of truth is escaping from you."

Toto laughed; he always believed Struve to be

jesting when in earnest, and in earnest when jesting. Then he sat watching De Nani, and wondering at his capacity for champagne.

"Cigars, cigars!" cried Pelisson, finishing his article with a dash, flinging down his pen and bursting out like a sun. "What's this? pudding!" He devoured it like a pig, and then roared again for cigars. Three boxes were swiftly passed in from the outside.

He placed one before him, sent his article off to the *Journal des Débats* office, which lies near by, and, leaning back in his chair with thumbs in the armholes of his waistcoat, blew clouds of smoke at the gilded ceiling, and cried: "Let's make a noise."

"What's up now?" inquired Toto.

"The Ministry will be down to-morrow!" cried Pelisson, flapping the sides of his chest with his turtle-fin hands. "You'll hear the tumble of portfolios—flip, flap, flop; and I've helped to pull them, ehu! Let us make a noise; it's the only thing worth living for. I'd die in a world where I couldn't make a noise; you couldn't make me a worse hell than a padded room. You, Toto—how do you live without making a noise? Gaillard squeaks in the *Revue des Deux Mondes*, Struve grumbles in the *Temps*, I roar in the *Débats;* you, wretched child! are silent: take up a pen or a paint-brush and make a noise."

" I would if I could," mourned Toto.

" You mean you could if you would!" retorted Pelisson. " Write a little book of poems, and I'll abuse them; I'll make your name rattle like a pea in a bottle. Write an ode to the Pope or paint a modest picture—there's two ideas for you gratis, each a fortune. Give me some coffee."

" I wouldn't give a pin for fame unless I earned it," said Toto, handing the coffee. " I'd just as soon swing a rattle as have a work of art of mine " —Struve groaned— " made famous by my friends or my position."

" Why," cried Pelisson, " he's talking sense, this boy is! "

" He's talking nonsense," said Struve.

" He's talking divinity—I mean (hic) divinely," said Gaillard, who was finishing his second bottle of champagne, and writing poetry on his cuffs with the stylographic pen that had just helped in the destruction of a Ministry.

De Nani was dumbly digesting; he had filled his pockets with cigars, and was wishing he had brought a sack. He was also drunk—in fact, to put it plainly, very drunk.

"I'm talking *sense*," cried Toto with flashing eyes.

"*He* can't paint," suddenly broke out De Nani, the drunkenness lifting like a veil and disclosing his true thoughts. "He's only pretending. Doesn't want to paint—'sgot four mistresses."

He slipped away from his chair as if sucked down by a whirlpool. A roar of laughter went up that shook the ceiling, and then, to everyone's horror, Toto the debonair, the hero of cock-fights and what not, broke into tears.

At this extraordinary sight Gaillard first gazed with a grin, and then burst out like a firework touched off, wringing his hands and calling upon God.

"Devil take that old scoundrel!" cried Pelisson, kicking at the body of De Nani, which seemed quite flaccid now that the truth had got out of it. " Where did you pick him up?—he's a scamp, he's a scamp!"

" Toto, my dear Toto," lisped Struve, " paint a picture to-morrow, and I'll make it famouth for you. So help me God! I will, or my name's not Struve."

" Alas!" cried Gaillard, drinking off a glass of brandy, " I am touched at the soul. Toto, my Toto, our Toto, *do* not grieve. I, too, will write a little poem, and it will make your picture famous. Where is that wretch? Kick him, Pelisson!"

" Don't let the waiters in," choked Toto. " It's only stupidity "—sniff, sniff—" the old fellow is drunk; don't kick him, P-P-Pelisson, he's an old man. I p-picked him up at my mother's; he's only stupid. There, I'm all right."

" Oh, dear me!" sighed Struve; " we are all right now, let us play baccarat."

" I am desolatéd," mourned Gaillard, who had now to be comforted. " And my little poem is spoiled." He looked at his shirt cuffs and broke into tears.

CHAPTER III.

WHEN Gaillard was at last comforted and set writing poems in a corner, the waiters were admitted, the table was cleared, and cards produced.

" Shall we go to the club? " asked Toto.

" No, play here," answered Struve.

They played loo, and Pelisson kicked the senseless body of De Nani, which had been pushed right under the table for propriety's sake, when luck went against him.

Toto played furiously, partly to drown the remembrance of his unmanly tears, partly to be successful. His eyes burned, his cheeks were like carnations, and his luck was frightful; but he played with the dogged determination peculiar to him in little things, the pig-headed obstinacy which, had it been allied with talent and poverty, might have landed him in the Ministry or Academy.

was awry. It was a cheerless party; Pelisson was
half asleep, and Toto as white as a ghost. Gaillard, his cuff scribbled over with lunatic poetry,
cast his mournful eyes at the dawn peeping in white
over the silent Boulevard des Capucines.

" I was once a youth," said Gaillard. " That is
what the world says to us in the dawn. The dawn
ever fills me with despair—a delicious despair. I
do not know why, but it seems forever linked to
that divine forlorn hope, love. This is the light
from which we rebuild old castles and recall vanished faces. In the faint wind that moves we hear
the whisper of voices. Fair women walk in vanished gardens, and the sound of the dew recalls
their tears."

" Ah!" cried De Nani, " is this a harp I hear, or
the voice of a mortal man? "

" Have you read my little poem," continued
Gaillard, " commencing,

> " O Love, whose every golden tress
> The sunshine holds of loveliness,
> What tragedy in what dark dawn
> Hath lent thine eyes such mournfulness?
> O—— "

"Oh, stop!" said Toto. "Your poetry makes me want to commit suicide."

"That," said Gaillard, "shows but the beauty of it. My ambition is to write a quatrain that will be as poisonous to hope as strychnine. Hope, that accursed allurement born of the—— Heaven! I am going to be ill; I have swallowed a bad oyster."

"Run to the window," commanded Toto.

"Brandy," suggested Pelisson.

"I am better," declared the poet. "The taste has passed. The question is, Will it prove poisonous? *Mon Dieu!* and the proofs of my 'Fall of the Damned' are not corrected."

"Never mind," said Toto gloomily. "You can correct them as you are falling. Oh, what a wretched world this is! I'm going to drown myself in the Seine." He rose, yawning, from his chair. "Who will follow me?"

"I will as far as the door," said Struve, rising also. "Pelisson, where are you for?"

"Home and go to bed," said Pelisson, rising also. "M. de Nani—why, he's drunk again!"

M. le Marquis de Nani had risen from his seat,

and seemed trying to walk upstairs through the air. It was the back blow of the night.

" I never saw a man slip into drink, like a girl into her shift, so swiftly and with such divine simplicity," lisped Struve. " Do wash his face, someone; he is painted like a *demi-mondaine*, and the paint has broken loose over his nose. Can't possibly take him into the street such a disgraceful figure."

They washed De Nani's face with white wine and Toto's handkerchief, whilst the old man struggled and resisted like a child. It was a mournful spectacle, and Toto did not laugh as the others did.

" That's what's the end of all," he thought. " Eugh! what a beastly thing life is! "

" Now put on his hat," commanded Pelisson, who acted as master of the ceremonies, " and jam it down—that's right. I will carry his cane. Drive him before you, and call a cab," he cried to the *garçon*, handing him a napoleon for *pourboire.*

They got the old man into a fiacre, weeping and

protesting and fighting like a lunatic with his keepers.

"Where shall we send him to?" asked Pelisson.

"I don't know where he lives; send him to the Morgue, send him to the Prefecture, send him anywhere you like," said Toto.

"I know," said Struve. "I have an enemy—he's a Legitimist; I'll send him a drunken Marquis for a present." And he gave the name and address of his enemy to the driver, with half a napoleon to pay the fare. "Get him into the house at any price," commanded Struve; "he's the father of the gentleman who lives there. There goes the old nobility."

He finished as the cab drove away, leaving a thin stream of curses on the morning air. And little did Toto dream where those curses would come to roost.

"What a jolly night we have had!" said Gaillard, as they parted at the corner of the Rue de la Paix.

"And we have all done something," said Pelisson. "You have written a poem,—don't have that shirt washed, they'll sell it in strips after you are dead,—and I have written my article, and Struve has made a present to his enemy of De Nani, who has made a beast of himself."

"And I," said Toto, "have made a fool of myself."

"That's what you were born for," said Pelisson. "But never mind, Toto, you make a most charming fool."

Then Toto found himself alone at the corner of the Rue de la Paix.

Some she-asses were passing, and he stopped the *auvergnat* driving them, and had a glass of milk, because that was *chic*, and when he had drunk the milk he wished he had not, because there was no one to look; and, besides, he was tired of being *chic*. Then, with the asses' milk still upon his lips, he came along down the Rue de la Paix in the direction of the river.

The change of his five-franc piece the *auvergnat* had given him mostly in copper; it bulged out his trousers-pocket, and made a clanking sound as he walked. Paris was waking up, the lidlike shutters of the shops were rising through a thousand streets; and as he passed through the Place Vendôme several early morning cabs laden with luggage from the Nord Station tore by.

In the Rue Castiglione he stopped. What should he do? It was too early to go home, too late for the club; the world he knew had gone to bed, the world he dimly knew of was waking up. A world in its shirt-sleeves, clean, bright, busy, and apparently happy. The dinner, the supper, the Marquis de Nani, Pelisson's roaring voice, Struve's lisp, and Gaillard's melancholic poetry, all pursued him like Eumenides of a low sort, impotent, yet able to tease.

On the Pont de Solferino he stood to look at the river, and might have thrown himself in had not the water looked so cold, and had he not remembered that he was unable to swim.

Then, turning back, he came along the arcade of the Rue de Rivoli, walking leisurely and listening to the birds singing in the trees of the gardens of the Tuileries.

The Place de la Concorde seemed horribly immense, and the far-away Eiffel Tower looked like a filmy giant straddling his legs, his hands in his pockets, and wearily waiting for something to do. Crossing the Place de la Concorde came a solitary girl carrying something in her hand; following the girl came a man.

CHAPTER IV.

THE POETRY OF HATS.

TOTO saw that the man was begging from the girl, and the girl was walking quickly. The man was a horrible-looking scoundrel.

"And here," said Toto, "is something to do."

He advanced rapidly and obliquely upon the pursued and pursuer, who, when he saw that the game was up, called out a vile word and turned to run. But he had reckoned without Toto.

It was all over in a minute, and from a distance it looked like a sparrow-fight, Toto in his brown tweeds, and the Barrier bully in his antique, rusty, long-tailed coat. The next our bully was running for his life towards the Pont de la Concorde, bawling and holding his nose, and the Prince, with his hat on the back of his head, was talking to the girl.

"Look!" cried Toto, screaming with laughter. "Three gendarmes are after him."

"Oh, monsieur!" murmured the girl,—she had blue eyes and the air of a fluttered dove,—"how can I thank you for having saved me?"

"Let us hurry away," said the Prince. "I see a gendarme shading his eyes at us over there. Let's dodge away down the arcade. Look! he's coming towards us. Run!"

They ran down the arcade hand in hand, to the wonder of the boys who were taking down the shop shutters. There was no earthly occasion for this flight. But Toto always embroidered upon a position; he could not behold a cat-fight without mentally suggesting betterments; besides, it was *outré*.

"Now we are safe," said he, as they turned up a by-street. "Oh, what fun! Tell me, mademoiselle, may I not carry your little parcel? No? May I not accompany you, then, to your journey's end?"

"Oh, yes!" said the girl. "My parcel is but a hat I am taking to M. Verral in the Rue St. Honoré. I do not live there, monsieur; I work for him at home. I live all alone in a little room near the Rue de Babylone—I and Dodor;" and she cast up her April-blue eyes as if through the rim of her hat she saw Dodor in the blue April skies, together with a vision of angels.

" Who is Dodor? " inquired Toto in a gruff and almost jealous voice.

" He is my lark," said the girl; and Toto brightened.

" You have a lark? "

" Oh, yes, monsieur; and if you could hear him sing! He brings the green fields to Paris in his voice."

" You keep him in a cage? " asked Toto, searching for conversation to fit a lark of this description, and not finding much.

" I keep him in a very big cage, monsieur. Ah! his cage ought to be the blue heavens; but, then, how could I hear him sing? I bought him in a little cage—not so big; but the parrot of Mme. Liard, our concierge, dying, I bought its cage— one, oh, so big; " and she measured the width of a wine-tun with hands that fluttered out like white butterflies, for Toto had wrested from her the parcel; also, she wore no gloves.

" Dear me! how funny!   And you call him Dodor.   This is Verral's, is it not?   Now, may I—
please don't think me rude—may I wait for you?
I have nothing to do—I mean, I want to hear more
about Dodor.   I cannot say ' mademoiselle '; it
sounds so stiff.   *My* name is To—Désiré Cammora."

" And mine, monsieur, is Célestin Sabatier.   I
will run in with the hat.   If I can see the forewoman, Mme. Hümmel, I will not detain you
long."

" Don't call me ' monsieur,' " said Toto; but she
had vanished.

It was an extraordinary find, this—a real live
Henri Murger grisette.   She might have stepped
out of " The Mysteries of Paris," without her cap,
of course, but even more charming in a hat.   She
was " all there," even to the lark in the parrot cage.
The parrot cage made him certain that the lark
was no trumped-up tale; she would never have
thought of inventing a parrot cage.   He remembered with a sort of satisfaction the poverty and
neatness of her dress.

Ten minutes passed, and then she came out again, like April after a cloud has passed, smiling, and with an air of triumph.

"Mme. Hümmel is so pleased, and I am so happy!" cried Célestin, as they walked away down the Rue St. Honoré, all beautiful with the morning. "She has given me an extra franc. Just think!" And she held out three in the pink shell of her palm.

"How much do you get for making a hat?" asked Toto.

"Two francs, and I find my own thread; but for this hat I have received three. It was an inspiration. Do you know, monsieur, that hats come to one? Sometimes I am perplexed. There lie all the materials,—the tulle, ribbons, flowers, what-not,—and there sit I, so like a stupid girl it seems impossible that I should make the hat—impossible as building the Eiffel Tower. And then, suddenly, something comes to me. I see the hat, and it is made. That is when I am stupid. At other times they come to me in hundreds—hats more beautiful than a dream; and, oh! if I had a hundred hands I

could find work for them all. Yesterday it was a
gloomy morning. Dodor drooped in his cage, and
I felt very dull. Then the sun broke out—you remember how beautifully—and Dodor sang, and the
blue sky looked in through the window and
brought me this hat like a gift from the good God.
Mme. Hümmel said it was April itself. And is it
not strange, monsieur, that the seasons should
help one so? For Spring helps me in her way, and
Summer and Autumn in their way, even Winter
a little,—and he helps few,—but of all of them I
like Spring the best," sighed Célestin, casting her
eyes up once more at the sky of her imagination
and the angels she seemed always to see there.

"I suppose people wear more hats in the
spring," was the reply of Toto to this revelation of
an artist's work, and for that reply he deserved
damning as an artist.

"Oh, yes," said Célestin. "The spring is the
time of all others; one makes more money in the
spring."

Toto had steered the way into the Rue du Mont
Thabor, a little street that lies parallel to the Rue

St. Honoré, and just behind the Hôtel Lille et Albion.

Here there was a *crémerie*, into which he invited her to enter. They took their seats at a little marble-topped table, which was soon spread with coffee, white bread, and butter.

Célestin quite cast away her reserve; she never had much, and what she had was that of a timid child. This creature, gentle as a bird, and thriving by her own quaint and lovely art in the midst of the great, white, cruel, beautiful city, was in herself a revelation—God, one might almost fancy, supporting her with his fingers as he supports the snowdrops above the snow; Art, one might almost fancy, turning from the Louvre and all its treasures, and smiling towards the Rue de Babylone and this humble slave interpreting her dreams by ribbon and tulle.

"I?" said Toto with his mouth full of bread and butter, and speaking in answer to a question of his companion. "I am an artist—a painter, you know."

Célestin lowered the cup she was raising to her

lips. He had won her admiration forever by beating the bully, and now he was an artist.

"I have never met one before," murmured
Célestin. "How great that must be, to be an
artist! I have seen them at the Louvre. I sometimes go to the Louvre; the rooms are so beautiful,
and the ceilings,"—the child evidently had her
limitations,—"and one sees such strange people—
English women in such strange hats. And do you
paint in the Louvre?"

"No, Célestin; I work in an atelier of my own."

Never before in the course of his brief artistic
career had praise thrilled him like this, the frank
and artless homage of a girl of eighteen who found
herself for the first time in her life in the presence
of a real artist; there were no ateliers in the street
off the Rue de Babylone, only workshops.

"At the Porte St. Martin," said Célestin,
"where sometimes Mme. Liard takes me,—she is
a friend of the doorkeeper, and sometimes he gives
her permits,—I have seen a very sad play. It was
about an artist: he was very poor—that is to say,
not so very poor at first, but he got poorer as the

play went on, and thinner, till at last his cheeks were like this." She sucked her cheeks in. "Then in the last act he tied a rope to a beam in the ceiling, and made a noose in the rope and put his head through it; I clung to Mme. Liard, I was so frightened. You cannot think how terrible it was till the door broke open and his father rushed in,—he was the son of a duke in disguise,—and the concierge came after, and a lot of people, and they cut him down. Everyone wept. There was a villain in the piece, and, oh! such a pretty girl," finished Célestin. "But I liked the artist best. Are all artists very poor, M. Désiré?"

"Oh, we manage to scrape along," said Toto, "when we can sell our pictures; we can't always do that—we can't always get them exhibited, even. I sent one last year to the Salon."

"The Salon—where is that?" asked Célestin.

"It's a picture show; they give prizes for the best pictures."

"And did your picture get a prize?"

"No," said Toto mournfully. "They would not even hang it on the walls—it was too classical, some people said; and one man, a man who ought to know, told me it was jealousy."

"Ah, *mon Dieu!* how terrible! It was so with the artist in the play: he was betrayed by a man who was jealous of him—oh, poor M. Désiré!"

"Célestin," said Toto, "do not call me monsieur; call me Désiré."

"Désiré," said Célestin, like an obedient child.

"That's right; and now tell me, Célestin, how comes it that you live all alone with this lark of yours."

"My mother died when I was so high," said Célestin, holding one hand three feet from the floor. "And I bought Dodor at the Halles Centrales; he cost three francs."

This was the history of her life as given by Célestin, with a mournful little gesture of the hands, as if to say "That's all."

"But," said Toto, "you must have found it very dull—I mean, you must have had to work for yourself; you have no brothers or sisters, have you? or cousins, or people of that sort?"

"Oh, no! I have always been alone; but people

are very good to me; I love the world—it is very good, and it is so beautiful. On Sundays, sometimes, I go with Mme. Liard to the Buttes Chaumont; I think heaven must be like that."

"Is that as far as you have been?"

"I have been to Champrosay once when I was very little. I can remember it still, but it is like a dream."

Toto was producing his coppers to pay the bill, and thinking how fortunate it was that the *auvergnat* had given him change in coppers, also how fortunate it was that he had bought the asses' milk, for these coppers were eminently in keeping with the struggling artist. He also kept his coat buttoned to hide his watch-chain, for Toto was now being driven by an idea half formed, yet fully potent, just as the asses had been driven up the Rue de la Paix by the man in sabots, armed with a stick.

Célestin drew out her little purse as if to help in the settlement of the account, and then put it back with a sigh of contentment at Toto's gesture. One could see her satisfaction at not having to part with her centimes, for she did not in the least try to hide it. She crossed herself and moved her lips as if giving thanks to the good God for the breakfast he had sent her, and then she cried, " Oh, how wicked I have been!"

"Why?" cried Toto, turning from a dispute about fifty centimes with the waiter.

" I have forgotten Dodor, and he has been waiting for his breakfast, and I—I have been thinking of other things."

She rose with the rapidity and grace only given to us when the knees are young. She seemed as if she must spread out a pair of wings and fly at once to Dodor. So Toto relinquished his fifty centimes and accompanied her. He proposed that they should take a cab.

"Oh, no!" cried Célestin, "that would be far too extravagant. I think you are very extravagant, mons—Désiré; as for me, I have never been in a cab."

"Never what?" said Toto.

"Never been in a cab. I always walk—sometimes I take the omnibus; but that is when it is wet, omnibuses are so expensive; but they are delightful. It is such fun seeing the people, and they are so friendly; I would like to spend all my life driving in omnibuses. Old gentlemen have often helped me out and walked home with me to see me safe."

" Good gracious! what do they say to you? "

" Three old gentlemen have seen me home," said Célestin. " And——"

" Three all together? "

" Oh, no! at different times; and one had a red rosette in his buttonhole."

" And what did they say to you? "

" That's the funny thing: they all wanted me to go to the theater, and of course I was delighted,— just imagine!—and we were to meet at different places; and then we talked of other things, and they all took such an interest in Dodor and asked so many questions all about how I lived; and one, the one with the red rosette, gave me a great five-franc piece—he said it was a present for Dodor. But the funny thing was, when we reached home they had forgotten about the theater, and said they had other engagements, and that they would come some other evening. The old gentleman with the rosette gave me another five-franc piece for myself, only this one was in gold, a very small one, and he told me to remember and always be a good girl, for the angels were watching me; and I said I would, and he kissed my hand and went away. But I never saw them again, for one never meets the same person twice in an omnibus, you know."

Toto assented. He was thinking of this lark that flew so mysteriously between Célestin and sin, and lived in a parrot cage.

They had crossed the Place de la Concorde by this, crossed the Pont de la Concorde, and were heading for the Eiffel Tower. They were walking quickly, too, for was it not to the relief of Dodor, pining for his groundsel, or whatever larks are fed upon?

The exercise began to tell upon Célestin. She oughed a little, and put her hand to her chest high p near the collar-bone.

" You are not strong? "

" Oh, yes, I am very strong, only my chest pains

me at times, and I cough at nights sometimes—a little, not much."

" Célestin," said Toto, in a very serious voice, " I want you to meet me again.   Will you? "

" Oh, dear! " sighed Célestin; " I forgot that we had to part."

" But we shall meet again."

" When? "

" Could you meet me to-morrow morning? "

" Yes."

" At eight? "

" Yes."

" At the corner just where the Champs Élysées joins the Place de la Concorde? "

" Yes—oh, yes!   And you will be there? "

" I will.   And, Célestin, look here: we are not rich, you know, and we ought to help each other. Look here."   He took out a handful of coppers and some silver pieces, all that he had remaining from the five-franc piece.   " We will divide, and take half each."

" No—oh, no! "

" Yes," said Toto, " you must."

" But you will want it."

" No, I shan't.   You want it more than I do.
Besides," continued the Prince, " I have not a lark
to keep up."

They divided, squabbling over an odd sou,
and when the accounts were settled they walked
on.

" How good you are!" said Célestin, almost in
tears at the manifold bounties God was heaping
upon her this fine April morning. " I will put it in
the money-box for Dodor. Oh, dear! why did I
think of dying just then? It must have been the
thought of Dodor. I often lie awake and think
what would become of him if I died. I have a
money-box for him to give to someone to be kind
to him in case I got ill and died. The five-franc
piece is in it, and other money as well. I will put
yours, too. See, this is where I live."

They had reached a gloomy street sprinkled with
a few shops, and filled with the boom of an adjacent
factory. A gloomy house of four stories was the
house where Célestin lived.

" Now I shall know where to find you in case

you fail to meet me to-morrow," said Toto, as they shook hands.

"I will not fail," she replied. "I have never broken a promise in my life—only once."

"When was that?"

"This morning, when I promised Dodor to be back in half an hour."

Then he kissed her hand just as the old gentleman with the red rosette had done, and wandered away, his head filled with thoughts of her. For it was a peculiarity of Célestin's that, whilst she must have appealed to the angels in heaven, she also appealed strongly to Porte St. Martin minds.

CHAPTER V.

GAILLARD THE COMFORTER.

THEN he went home, and bathed and dressed and said " The club " when his mother, in *peignoir* and morning paint, asked him where he had spent his night with that good, dear Marquis de Nani. Later in the day he wandered into Struve's rooms.

" Go away, Toto," said Struve, who was busy writing at his table. He supplied seven journals with his ideas, from the *Fremdenblatt* to the *Figaro*, and he seemed now engaged in writing for the whole seven at once. One could see nothing of the lisping, melancholy Struve of the night before in this lightning scribe. " Go away. I have no time for Totos. Come in three hours' time."

" What are you at? " inquired Toto, sinking into a chair and lighting a cigarette.

" Praising a man I hate."

" See here: stop writing your gibberish for five minutes; I want to speak to you."

Struve took out his watch and laid it on the table.

" I am listening."

" You once said that if a man of talent were to start in Paris with three thousand francs and his ten fingers,—those were your words,—that if he did not get on he deserved to fail."

" So he does; what more? "

" I have been thinking of having a try, working like a devil, and kicking over all this absurdity."

" Do; it won't do you any harm. What at— politics? "

" Oh, you owl! " cried Toto. " Politics—what do I care for politics! Art, that's the only thing I care a button for. I'm going to dress in a blouse, and work like a common man—make my name off my own bat, as they say in England. I'm utterly sick of doing nothing; I must move—I must." And Toto moved his arms. " And I am tied; no one takes me seriously. Look at old De Nani, praising me one moment, and then the next—— Faugh! I'm a Prince; I am worth ten million francs when my mother dies. I play with art, that's enough for people; they don't see my work, they see me."

"You are always so much in evidence," said Struve. "That's where the mischief is; you cut such antics that people have no time to observe your serious attempts. You have got a frightful lot of energy, and you are a Prince—that's what is wrong with you; you must be doing, you are tired of the club, the Bois, cock-fighting at Chantilly. By the way, I see your name in the *Figaro* this morning under a thin disguise—Longchamps and all the rest of it. Your volcano is bunged up by ennui; you want a new opening for the lava to escape. Well, take my advice: move in the plane of least resistance; buy a coffee mill and grind it."

"Do be serious," said Toto; "I come to you as a friend."

"Toto," said the critic, "I am very serious, else I would not advise you to leave art alone. What's the use? This, great, beautiful Moloch wants a whole life to eat, or nothing. There are a thousand men in Paris who have flung their all into

this furnace. What will come out of all this forlorn thousand? Half a dozen, and they will be
filled with despair. The walls of the Musée de
Louvre are painted with the blood of men, and
that's success. What of the failures? Their story
would shock creation. Art lives on failures; they
keep the paint shops going, and serve as a background to three or four stars. Now go away.
God in heaven! it's four, and the post for Germany
goes out at six."

"You are never so stupid as when you are serious," blurted out Toto, as he rose and flung his
cigarette-end into the grate.

But Struve did not even answer; he was writing
away.

Toto then met the young Prince de Harnac, who
invited him to dine at the Mirlitons; he refused,
alleging a headache. Then he called on Pelisson,
and found him out. He was wearily entering the
Place de l'Opéra, when the devil flung him into
the arms of Gaillard.

Gaillard's collar seemed higher than ever, and he
had a distracted air.

"I am running about looking for my dinner," said Gaillard. "That infernal De Brie has gone off to his country house, and forgotten my check and left me to starve. I will turn an editor, and write no more poetry nor little articles for his journal. Dear Toto, come and give me my dinner, and lend me a thousand francs, and comfort me. Sit here with me, and have an absinthe, and look at Paris as it passes; and then we will go to the Maison Dorée and dine."

"You are just the man I want," said Toto, as they took their seats at a café, where the marble-topped tables had ventured out now that the weather was fine, and even a bit warm. "I want your help and advice. I've been with that villain Struve, and he has depressed me, and flung cold water on me."

"Struve is a critic," said Gaillard in a vicious voice; "he is one of the sorrows of art. I do not know what criticism is coming to. Have you seen that article in the *Tribune* on Mallarmé?—Mallarmé, that divine shadow moving in the twilight of the gods, even he is not safe from their mud.

But what is this, Toto, you say about help and advice? Are you being worried by some woman? Is your mother tormenting? Unfold yourself to me."

"Look here, Gaillard: you are a man of sense, you have sympathy. I am sick of life, living like a cabbage, and I want to live really, I want to be famous without the assistance of anyone; I have a talent."

"You have an undoubted genius."

"And I want to use it. I go to Struve, and he sneers at me, tells me to grind a coffee mill."

"Oh, that Struve!" mourned Gaillard. "What led you to a critic for advice or sympathy? He told you to grind a coffee mill? Give me a cigarette, Toto; my case is empty; I will take three. He told you that! They fancy their cheap wit kills, these critics do; but you are not alone, Toto. Did you see the critique on my little poem 'Satanitie' in the *Écho de Paris?* Well, that is what they fling nowadays at an artist, and call it wit. But Pelisson is replying by a counterblast in the *Débats.* Dear old Pelisson! He knows no more of poetry than a rhinoceros; but he roars, and he has reduced the art of slaying a critic to a fine edge."

"Yes, yes," said Toto, trying to lead Gaillard from himself for a moment; "but what do you think of my plan? I am going to take an attic and work in a blouse—I *am;* and, besides, do you know, Gaillard, I have met the most charming girl. She lives in an attic on three sous a day with a lark; she trims hats, and she has eyes just the color of Neapolitan violets. I have never loved a woman before."

"You love her?" cried Gaillard, "and you would leave the world for her to live in an attic? Oh, *mon Dieu!* what a romance you might make of life! And is that idea all your own? *Mon Dieu!* you, a Prince, rich and young and charming, beloved by all the women of Paris—the very entry of such an idea into your brain proclaims you an artist. It is like the Prince in my little forest tale who renounced the world for a wood-nymph— my little tale called ' Nymphomanie.' You have read it."

"No, I haven't."

" But I gave you a copy."

" Oh, yes, I remember now—the nymph who turned into a sow. It was a beautiful story; but never mind it for a moment. Tell me, Gaillard: you are not saying that just to please me?"

" I," said Gaillard; " I am charmed with the idea, the originality of it, the color of it. It has a perfume of violets—those violets that come in autumn as if to increase the sadness of the withered leaves. De Musset might have written a play upon it. I, ha! I will—I will write a poem on it."

" For goodness' sake, don't!" said Toto in alarm. "I want no one to know. With my blouse I become a man like other men; I give myself a year, and then—we will see what Otto Struve and De Nani say."

" But you are not serious, Toto?" cried Gaillard, who was now the man alarmed, for Toto was a little income to him, a cigarette mine, and a most joyous companion. "You would die, my child, under the hardships of such a life; you were not born to the blouse, you were born to the purple."

" I am serious!" cried the Prince, greatly exas-

perated; "you are as bad as the rest of them.   You
are——"

"I am not; *mon Dieu!* do not freeze me, Toto,
with that face.   I was but thinking of your health;
you have cast frost upon me, and I was feeling so
happy; besides, a garret may be made most comfortable—it may indeed: you can have a little char-
coal-fire when the weather is cold, and a garret
need not be ugly.   I saw an old oak chest in the
Rue Normandie to-day; it cried out to me to buy it,
but I had not the money; we will buy it to-morrow.
We will not have the walls papered; most have,
but we need not be vulgar though we are poor.
Oh, Toto, poverty is a romance if it is taken in the
right way; we will teach the poor how to endure
their poverty romantically.   No, we will not have
paper—plain plaster and an etching or two of
Albrecht Dürer's, a little library confined to one
bookshelf.   Loti, Baudelaire, and a few mystics;
a lark to sing to one whilst one paints or writes; a
girl with blue eyes to love; a pipe to smoke—what
more does one want?   In the name of Heaven,
what more does one want?   I call upon Heaven to

witness. I think the problem of modernity solved in the one word 'simplicity.' We are too be-scented, embroidered, and diffuse; we eat too much and love too broadly; we want concentration. Genius is like a burning-glass; it must be focused so that the rays come together in a narrow point, else the rays will not burn. I saw a stove in bronze of Henri Quatre; we will get that—it's in the same place, Rue de Normandie. Did you see that girl pass by? She pulled up her dress to show me her ankles; they were like cow heels. Some people have no discretion; they show what they ought to hide, and hide what they ought to show. I have noticed it in everything, even conversation. Well, we will get the stove and some other things—it will be like making a nest; and when all is ready you will spread out your wings and sing, and the female bird will come. Heavens! I know just the place you want, in the Rue de Perpignan. I have a friend there, a genius, but very weird; they call him Fanfoullard, no one knows his real name. He is one of the mysteries of Paris; he subsists by painting fans, and will not get out of bed till dusk;

he says inspirations come to him only when he is in bed. That necessarily imposes limitations on his art, but his fans are poems; he spreads them with autumn and spring, and sends them fluttering over the world; he dreams of the beautiful women who will use them as he lies there unknown in his bed. Life is full of poetry; we find it in the most unexpected places. Well, the room below that of Fanfoullard is unlet—it was so, at least, a week ago; we will take it; it has a little room adjoining that will do for a bedroom. We will go hunting for the furniture, you and I, to-morrow."

" But, see here, Gaillard: I am not playing at this, and I must be economical. I'm going to start on three or four thousand francs, and make that do. I'm deadly in earnest."

" You are right," said the poet. " It would be absurd to live in an attic with a bank-book; besides, you can always apply to your mother, Mme. la Princesse, should the wolf scrape too loudly at the door."

" Oh, good gracious, you will drive me mad! If I don't succeed I will hang myself; I would never

have the face to come back; and what I mean by
success is, success without help. I am stiff with
sitting still and being waited upon; I want to *be*."

And Toto's eyes gleamed madly in the gaslight,
whilst Gaillard felt a decided shiver. Then he
remembered Toto's .general eccentricities, and
rubbed his chin, making his thin beard crackle.·
" It will last a month," thought he; " and then we
shall all drive home in a cab very hungry, and the
Princesse will kill the fatted calf, and the girl will
be pensioned."

" Gaillard, what are you thinking of? " demanded Toto.

" I was thinking that I should like to be young
again like you," burst out Gaillard, a lot of lunatic
ideas waking up and dancing like Bacchantes
around the lie. " And be loved by a beautiful girl,
and work for her, and fail, and die in her arms;
those are the happiest lives, after all, failure ending
in death with one's beloved. Success ruins one's
life. I have never been happy since I met it, when
I was young; but I was never young, I sucked
nepenthe with my mother's milk. I do not believe

I was ever born; I was found in some field of poppies, and they hid the fact. When I have written
my last song I shall drop in some field of poppies.
Ah, me, wretched body of mine! Toto, let us go
and dine and forget ourselves; let us become beasts
for an hour, and then you will come to my rooms.
Fanfoullard may be there; he always crawls out at
dark and rides to the Rue de Rivoli in an omnibus
with his eyes shut, for fear of seeing the terrible
people who make use of those vehicles. They put
him out in the Rue de Rivoli, and he opens his
eyes. Should he have any fans finished, he takes
them to Nadar, who monopolizes his work; then
he always comes to my rooms and smokes—I leave
tobacco for him on the mantel. He is my familiar. For days sometimes we do not meet, when
I happen to be out, but I always know that he has
been; he leaves a smell of withered flowers behind
him. All my greatest poems are due to Fanfoullard. You remember, Schiller could never
compose without rotten apples in his desk. Fanfoullard is my rotten apple. Come, let us go to the
Maison Dorée."

They rose from their seats and made languidly for the Boulevard des Italiens, Gaillard pausing at several toy shops to look in and admire the wares. In the Avenue de l'Opéra, at Brentano's window, a little volume of poems by Verlaine called to him to buy it, and as he had no money Toto bought it for him. He carried the book tight clasped to his chest as they wandered along to the Maison Dorée, where they entered and dined.

CHAPTER VI.

FANFOULLARD, MIRMILLARD, AND PAPILLARD.

Two hours later they came out, each smoking a big cigar; Gaillard's held delicately between finger and thumb and whiffed at occasionally, Toto's stuck in the corner of his mouth.

"Let us to the Moulin Rouge," said Gaillard. "I have dined; I want to laugh."

"But how about this Fanfoullard?"

The poet had quite forgotten Fanfoullard, the attic, the Henri Quatre stove, and all the rest of it.

"Oh, he will wait; Fanfoullard is eternal, like a tortoise. A hundred years hence you will find him painting his fans and crawling out at dark to sell them."

"But I don't want him in a hundred years; I want him now, to arrange about that room."

"What room?"

"The room you spoke of."

Gaillard groaned. He thought his companion

had forgotten all that, which showed that he only knew Toto by his surface.

" You will not find Fanfoullard interesting."

" Don't want to; but he will find me interesting, for I will pay him to see about the place and have it cleaned up."

" But Fanfoullard——" said the poet, stopping to scratch his head, for there was no Fanfoullard; he was a mythical creature that had escaped through one of the cracks in Gaillard's skull; he had never lived in the Rue de Perpignan, nor journeyed forth to sell fans in the dark with his eyes shut for fear of the frightful people one sees in omnibuses. It seemed almost a pity. " But Fanfoullard——" said his creator. " Ah, well; yes, let us go to my rooms and see if he has arrived."

They made for the Rue de Turbigo, for Gaillard condescended to live in the Rue de Turbigo. Here he kept his Muse, or, to speak more correctly, she kept him, assisted by Toto, Pelisson, Struve, De Brie the editor, and a host of others.

" Tell me about this Fanfoullard," asked Toto. " Is he a respectable sort of person? "

"Oh, eminently. My dear Toto, why walk so fast? I shall have indigestion."

"He doesn't practice on the violin or come in drunk, does he?"

"Never. Toto, tell me about this charming girl who has taken your heart; tell me her name?"

"Célestin."

"Ah, *mon Dieu!* Célestin! What a name!— full of light."

"Would you like to see her? Well, come to-morrow morning. I am going to meet her in the Champs Élysées at eight, and I'll tell you what: we will all go and breakfast together, and then we will take a trip into the country. You will do for a chaperon; you can watch about and meet us as if by accident—will you?"

"Why, yes," chirruped Gaillard, a vista of pleas-ure in the country, champagne, pretty girls, and April skies springing up before him, painted upon the night. "I shall be charmed. The country now is like a picture—the skies by Fantin, the blos-soms by Diaz. I will come in a straw hat. Tell me, Toto: shall I bring a girl?"

"Confound it, no!" said the Prince.   "Célestin is not that sort."

Gaillard sighed.

They had reached the house in the Rue de Turbigo where he lived, and passed through the entresol and up, up, up a great many stairs, for the poet lived at the top of his tree.

"Fanfoullard has not come, then," he cried in a voice of disappointment as he opened his door and revealed a big room lit by the remains of a fire. "Light a candle, Toto, whilst I build up the fire."

"There are no candles," said Toto, hunting about match in hand.

"True—I forgot," cried the poet, running into the little bedroom adjoining and returning with a night-light in a soap-dish; "I used them all to-day."

"Why, you don't burn candles in the daylight?"

"Indeed," said Gaillard, "I do. When I am working I always close the shutters and work by candlelight. My ideas are like moths; daylight dispels them, candlelight attracts them. They are like gray moths, the color of decay; could you look

in when I am at work, you would perhaps see them
flitting about my head—reveling around their
maker. *Bon Dieu!* this bellows is broken. Toto,
hand me that bundle of wood. I have written by
a night light. 'Satanitie' was written by a night-
light, finished in the first rays of the dawn; that
book was written at a single sitting in one night of
sheer madness."

"I know; you told me so the other day," replied Toto, whilst Gaillard, his hat still on his head,
and his frock-coat hanging round him like a skirt,
squatted on his hams before the fire, putting
pieces of stick upon it with finger and thumb,
whilst the flames leaped up and, assisting the feeble
flame of the night-light, illuminated the room.

The carpet was blue, the tablecloth red, the curtains maroon rep. Sundry German engravings
adorned the walls. One represented an angel in a
long chemise, saying, evidently, "Coosh!" to a
lion in a den, whilst Daniel, with a head four sizes
too large, stood by with an air of attention. Another, Tobias being haled along by an angry-look-
ing seraph to the music of cherubs playing upon

wooden harps and seated upon woolen clouds. Another, Ananias dying apparently of strychnine. There were three photographs on the mantel: one of a boy in plaid trousers clasping to his breast a wooden horse; another of a young man, wild of eye, and dressed in the uniform of the 101st of the line; a third, of a poet holding a little book in his hand. All three portraits were of Gaillard—Gaillard at ten, Gaillard at twenty-five, and Gaillard at thirty, as we know him.

In a bookshelf close to the mantel stood a volume of Schopenhauer, Baudelaire's "Fleurs de Mal," and ten volumes by Gaillard—that is to say, two volumes of each of his works; twinlets delicately bound, some gay as grisettes, but "Satanitie" ash-colored, with a black devil dancing on its back.

"Why," said Toto, glancing at Daniel, "do you keep those odious prints in your room?"

"I don't keep them," said Gaillard, rising with a distracted air, and wiping his fingers on his coat. "My poverty keeps them; they are part of the furniture. Look at the carpet, look at the curtains

—what a background! I am like a butterfly pinned to an outrageous tapestry, an indecent arras; they are my cross. I took them up with the rooms. Why do I remain in the rooms? They are haunted, Toto, by a man called Mirmillard. He was an opium-eater, and lived by writing for the *Quartier Latin.* You know the *Quartier Latin?* It is a *farouche* little journal of sixteen pages or so, and appears monthly, or is it quarterly? He blew his brains out just where you are sitting now; the hole was extant in the wall a month ago, but I had it stopped up with plaster. Have I seen his ghost? many times; it is one of my inspirations, and that is why I endure those terrible curtains, that terrible carpet, and, ah, *mon Dieu!* those terrible pictures. Toto, lend me your cigarette case; I will take three, and make you some coffee—I have all the *implementa* in this cupboard. Fanfoullard is not coming, it seems. No matter; I will seek him to-morrow myself. To-night perhaps, if we are lucky, we may see Mirmillard. He appeared to me only three nights ago, and the gash in his throat gaped."

" I thought you said he blew his brains out? "

" He completed the work with a razor," said Gaillard, putting the little kettle on to boil. " But enough of Mirmillard. These cigarettes are very good. Let us talk of flowers."

" Oh, bother flowers! " said the Prince, lying luxuriously back on the old sofa, whose springs were bursting out below. " Tell me, Gaillard; have you ever been in love with a woman? "

Gaillard, squatting before the fire, looked at the kettle with an expression as though he were regarding the gash in Mirmillard's throat. He had never seen that gash, simply because there was no Mirmillard, not even the ghost of one. He, like Fanfoullard, was one of Gaillard's creatures, born to bedizen conversation.

He made no response to Toto's question.

" For I am," said Toto, without waiting for one. " I never thought I should be; but that girl's eyes are quite different from other women's. But you will see her yourself to-morrow. Deuce! what is this? "

A little bundle of papers was disturbing his rest

on the sofa. He picked them out. They were newspaper cuttings, paragraphs about an individual called Papillard. For the last few months a series of little stories had been attracting the attention of Paris to the pages of *Gil Blas.* They were naughty, but screamingly funny, and just long enough to read whilst smoking a couple of cigarettes or sipping a glass of absinthe. They were signed " Papillard." Everyone was asking who Papillard was. Nobody knew but the editor, and editors never speak when they are told not.

" Why, hello! " cried Toto. " Do you know Papillard? "

" No," said Gaillard, removing the kettle from the fire in a hurry.

" But see here: here are things about him, addressed to him and opened."

" Oh," said Gaillard, " I know. He's a friend of Fanfoullard's. He must have been yesterday, and no doubt left them. My dear Toto, do you like your coffee strong? "

Gaillard's hand was shaking. He dared not admit that Papillard was himself. No one had ever

guessed it, for Gaillard, though a source of great
humor, was believed to be utterly destitute of that
quality, and so, in fact, he was. Papillard was a
sprite that lived in the brain of his unwilling host.
He was a creature like Fanfoullard and Mirmillard,
only much more highly organized, for he was able
to cling to his tenement and to exercise his abilities
in literature. The stories of Papillard horrified his
master when in print. There was something so
abominably low about them. Servant girls giggled
over them on back-stairs. Gaillard admitted to
himself in secret that he wrote them, and enjoyed
writing them, but he would sooner almost have
died than admitted the authorship. One of the
stories in question had for motive a cold leg of mutton. There is nothing particularly funny about a
cold leg of mutton, but the story was killing. And
it had been written by the author of " Satanitie "!
Gaillard, when he remembered this fact, felt dizzy,
and pinched himself to see if he was there. He
was jealous, too, of Papillard's fame. Wind of
these trifles had even reached England, or, at least,
the *Daily Telegraph.* " Satanitie " had never gone

so far.　When people cried " What a droll fellow
this Papillard is! " Gaillard's tongue had to lie mute
at the bottom of his mouth—a cruel torture.　You
cannot be two people at once.　You cannot be a
mystical poet, and a buffoon—at least, before the
eyes of the world.　He had discovered his genius
by accident, and too late.　His self-love had crys-
tallized round poetry, and, in fact, the poet was the
true *him*.　Papillard was a clove of garlic in a bon-
bon box, placed there by accident or freak, smelt
by everyone, but never localized.

He would have burnt Papillard's stories, but
they brought him money—much more money than
" Satanitie " or " Nymphomanie " or " The Poi-
soned Tulip " or " The World Gone Gray " had
ever brought him; and Gaillard was a sieve for gold
—at the mercy of every woman he met, who
robbed him of the money that ought to have gone
to his tailors, bootmakers, hatters, and hosiers.
Lately, indeed, he would have gone very much to
pieces only for the fantastic labors of Papillard, and
for these benefits he was ungrateful.　You know
the maxim of Rochefoucauld.

He handed Toto his coffee, and, to turn the conversation, reminded him of the loan of a thousand francs which he had requested on their first meeting that evening.

" It is indispensable to me," said Gaillard.

" I will let you have it," replied the Prince, " but not now. If you had money now, you would be off to the Moulin Rouge, and I should not see you in the morning. I will let you have it to-morrow evening when we come back."

" But I have not a centime! " cried Gaillard, turning out his waistcoat pockets in despair. " And how can I meet you, how can I get to the rendezvous, in this condition? "

" It's better for you to come like that than come, perhaps, tipsy. Besides, I will pay all expenses, and I will give you five francs now; that will pay your cab to the Champs Élysées in the morning. Stay at home and write poetry just for to-night, and think of all the fun you will have to-morrow night."

" *Mon Dieu!* " said Gaillard, as the vision of the Moulin Rouge vanished before him into thin air.

Part II.

CHAPTER I.

IT IS NOT ALWAYS MAY.

THE next morning broke fair. The sky over Paris held the blue of forget-me-nots, and the wind from the west, lazy and warm, ruffled the lilac of the Seine with streaks of sismondine. It was the summer end of April; she had still five days' tenancy, and here May had arrived before her time, flushed and warm from her journey, but seemingly unspeakably happy.

" Ah, *mon Dieu!* 'tis like an old Italian picture! " cried Gaillard as he opened his lattice in the Rue de Turbigo.

" Oh, *ciel!* " cried Célestin far away near the Rue de Babylone, as she stood by her open window and clasped her hands before all this beauty, whilst Dodor gave praise from the parrot cage till the brown sparrows, grubbing in the street below, cocked their impudent heads on one side, as if to say " What's that? Who is making that noise? "

Célestin had been dreaming of Toto, and praying before she slept that the morrow might be fine and that he would not forget. What a day had come in answer to her prayers! She fully believed that her prayers had brought this angelic morning, tripping with blue parasol outspread across the fields of light, across the hills of dreams and the country of impossible primroses. Then the artist turned from the window and from heaven, and flung herself into a hat.

It had got the better of her yesterday. She had stared vainly at the foundation. Nothing came, only the vision of Toto beating the beggar man, Toto drinking his coffee, Toto declaring himself an artist, Toto's eyes, Toto's nose, the coat he had worn, his beautiful hands, his hair so well groomed, his white teeth, and his angelic smile. You cannot put these things into a hat—that is to say, immediately; but now, after twenty-four hours nearly had elapsed, the miracle was accomplished.

The result was a confection that made Princesse

Klein look ten years younger at the Countess
Prim's garden party. She did not know that she
was wearing Toto upon her head, Toto idealized
and converted into a hat by the joint endeavors of
love and April, assisted by the fingers of Célestin
Sabatier.

The doing of it took but an hour, and then she
held it out on the point of her finger and smiled;
Dodor broke into a song of triumph, and the little
American clock on the shelf struck seven.

So she breakfasted—a cup of milk and a Vienna
roll eaten in haste—and gave Dodor his morning
fly round the room. Then she started, closing the
door carefully for fear of Mme. Liard's cat, and all
the way down the steep and dusty stairs Dodor's
voice pursued her, seeming to cry "Come back!
come back!"

Toto had dressed himself in his oldest suit of
tweed; he wore also a revolutionary-looking felt
hat. A Prince cannot break into a blouse in one
morning any more than a tree can cast its leaves in
one night, but he was advancing. He had also
been waiting since ten minutes to eight—that is to

say, exactly five minutes—for at five minutes to
eight Célestin appeared beneath the trees of the
Avenue Champs Élysées, and Toto, who had been
standing close to one of the little kiosks, came to
meet her.

She wore a bunch of blue violets in her bosom,
an artless adornment bought for a sou at the corner of the Rue de Varennes. She was in exactly
the same dress as that she had worn on the previous
morning, but her hands were gloved in honor of
Toto.

They shook hands and laughed a little, and inquired after each other's health. Then Toto led
her to some chairs placed close to one of the little
kiosks.

"Don't let us sit on those," said Célestin; "they
charge for them. I once sat on a little chair just
here, and a man came out and asked me for a sou;
there was nothing to be done but pay him."

"Never mind," said the Prince; "let us be extravagant for once in our lives. Célestin, I have a
treat for you—guess what it is."

Célestin thought vaguely of what it could be;

she could imagine nothing but a breakfast, hot rolls and butter and coffee, but somehow she did not care to tell of this imagining. She shook her head.

" I am going to take you for a day in the country and show you the flowers and things—that is, if you will come. Will you come, Célestin? "

" Oh, Désiré! " cried the girl. She could say no more; she held out both hands to Toto; her soul was in a tumult, and her eyes filled with tears of pure delight. The country, the mysterious country, the long-dreamt-of country, that land of her dreams compounded of old visions of Champrosay and the shrill sweetness of Dodor's song! Had Israfel appeared before her offering a trip to the fields of heaven, I doubt if his offer would have been received with such delight.

Toto felt an extraordinary little thrill run through him as he took her hands. No one had ever called him Désiré before in a voice like that; women, when they knew him well enough, always called him Toto, generally with a little laugh—men too. Here was a being, lovely and lovable, who called him by his right name, and, oh, with what sweetness! It was a new revelation of himself; it was as if, glancing in a mirror, he saw, reflected in a new way, a face very much more handsome and manly than his own, and yet the true reflection of his face. He would have loved that mirror and disliked the false mirrors he had been accustomed to, just as he was beginning to love Désiré—I mean Célestin. He kissed each little hand and put them back in her lap, where they rested as if satisfied.

" But where shall we go? " asked Toto, glancing round to see if he could make out any sign of Gaillard, and almost hoping that he had overslept himself.

" Oh, anywhere," said she. " What matter where, so that it is the country, where the trees are and the flowers? There is nothing so beautiful in the whole world as the trees; I dream of them sometimes, and they are lovely. Oh, see that white butterfly, white as an angel of heaven! he seems so glad, and he seems to know."

" Bother! " said Toto.

"What?" asked Célestin, coming back from heaven.

It was Gaillard in the distance. The poet had dressed himself for pastoral pleasures; he wore a gray frockcoat, a white waistcoat, and a straw hat —one of those straw hats they manage better in France: it was soft, and the brim curled. He had also a green necktie, to be in keeping with the grass, a rose in his buttonhole, and a large stick with a crook handle.

"Ah, my dear Désiré!" screamed the poet when in speaking distance. He had been schooled over-night to forget the odious little name Toto. "I despaired of seeing you; you were not to be seen, and now I find you sitting on a seat." He removed his hat and bowed low to Célestin.

"This is my friend M. Gaillard, the famous poet," said Toto, putting in "the famous poet" as a sort of excuse for the gayety and *bizarrerie* of his friend's dress, which he felt might frighten Célestin. But Célestin was not in the least frightened, though somewhat awed by the grandeur and white waistcoat of Gaillard. She had heard Mme. Liard speak of poets, wonderful and fabulous beings who lived in the country. The country seemed coming to her in bounds, the gods descending in showers, the birds singing louder in the trees of the Champs Élysées as if to welcome God Gaillard. She felt very happy.

"I am char-r-r-med," said Gaillard, bowing again and sinking into a chair. "Charmed to make Mlle. Célestin's acquaintance. I have not been to bed. To—Désiré, I have passed the night pen in hand; the dawn came in upon me as I worked; then it was too late."

He told this frightful lie with unction, for he had been, not only in bed, but snoring, when Mme. Plon, the concierge, tipped overnight by Toto, had actually come into his room and threatened to strip the clothes off him if he did not get up to go and meet Prince Cammora.

"*Mon Dieu*, monsieur!" had cried Mme. Plon. "Where will you get that hundred and ten francs you promised me for the rent but yesterday, should you fail to meet M. le Prince, and put His Highness in a bad temper?"

"How wonderful that is," said Célestin timidly, "to be a poet!"

Gaillard swelled a bit under his white waistcoat; then he laughed a dreary little laugh.

"Ah, mademoiselle, on a morning like this, yes, it is a wonderful thing to be a poet; but the world is not always May, the world is not always May. Mademoiselle has, perhaps, never read my——"

"No, of course she hasn't," cut in Toto. "At least—but that's not the question; tell me, where shall we go? We want a pleasant day. Now, what do you suggest?"

"But, mademoiselle——"

"She has already suggested anywhere; she is indifferent."

"Well," said Gaillard, who had the day's festivity already sketched out in his head, "I would propose a *petit déjeuner* now, then drop in to the Louvre and look at the Primitives, then I would propose *déjeuner*. After that, why not let us go to Montlhéry; we can take the train from the Gare d'Orléans. There is an old tower at Montlhéry that I love. We will dine at the Chat

Noir; they have some very fine carp in a pond
there, we will get the landlord to kill one and cook
it for us. He knows me, and he manufactures a
most delicious white wine sauce for carp. Well,
then we will have a carriage back and supper at
Foyot's, in the Rue de Tournon."

"That might do for M. Rothschild, but it is not
simple enough for us," said Toto, making sup-
pressed grimaces at the poet. "If I had sold a
picture even lately, but I haven't." A blank look
began to overspread Gaillard's face; he had not
reckoned on this. "So we must be very economical. How much money have you?"

"I have nothing!" cried the unfortunate Gaillard, and he began, as was his wont, to turn his
pockets inside out; then he remembered Célestin.
"My publisher was out when I called upon him.
My dear To— Désiré, how much have you?"

"Nineteen francs," said Toto with a diabolical
grin as he produced his money, "and a sou."

Célestin laughed and felt in her pocket for her
little shabby purse, but Toto said "No."

"We are rich. Poets and painters, you know,

Célestin, have a way of getting along on air, like the birds—haven't we, Gaillard?" But Gaillard only made a noise like a groan. "I know what we'll do. But first come, and we will have our *petit déjeuner* at the little *crémerie* in the Rue du Mont Thabor. You remember the *crémerie* where we breakfasted yesterday, Célestin?"

"That delicious little *crémerie!*" murmured Célestin, and they started.

They crossed the Place de la Concorde, Célestin laughing, Toto talking, and Gaillard walking silent like a froward child. He would have returned to the Rue de Turbigo had he not been absolutely penniless, for the five francs had all vanished, devoured by a rose, a cigar, and a cab.

"I will be silent," thought Gaillard, "and spoil this wretched Toto's pleasure; I will turn his feast into a funeral. Nineteen francs, *mon Dieu!* and three people, and a day in the country! The mind revolts!"

But ten minutes later he was calling for honey, declaring that he could not eat his roll and butter without it, and joining in the conversation. He could no longer endure the agony of holding his tongue; besides, he remembered the thousand francs Toto had promised him if he conducted himself decorously and with discretion.

"I know where we will go!" cried the Prince.

"Barbizon?" queried Gaillard, putting six lumps of sugar in his coffee.

"No, Montmorency; the chestnut trees will look splendid to-day. They are not in flower yet; but no matter—one cannot have everything."

"True," said Gaillard, trying to ogle Célestin and failing, for she was entirely engrossed with Toto and the bread and butter; "one cannot have everything. We will go to Montmorency, and sit beneath the chestnut trees and tell each other fairy tales."

"Oh, how delightful!" murmured Célestin.

"I will tell you the tale of the giant and the dwarf," resumed Gaillard. "It is my own—one of a series of *fin-de-siècle* fairy tales I am writing for Lévy. There is a terrible battle in it, and the giant beats the dwarf. In the olden tales the dwarf beats the giant invariably, but I have changed all that.

The giant in my story is the type of sin; he pelts the dwarf with roses, nothing more; the dwarf replies with mud; he is Virtue, and has a hump, and is hairy. Rousseau had a châlet at Montmorency; it is there still. I will leave you two amongst the primroses whilst I go and cast a stone at it—wretched man, murderer of his own children, destroyer of the *haute noblesse*, progenitor of the bourgeoisie!"

"Oh, bother Rousseau!" cried the Prince, helping Célestin to more honey. "We don't want to think of him; we want to be happy."

"True," said Gaillard; "you are young—we are all young; May is coming in. Désiré, a great idea has struck me: we will have a picnic. The inn at Montmorency may not be a good inn; I have my doubts about it. My children, listen to me: we will dine on the grass beneath those chestnut trees."

"But——" objected Toto.

"Hear me out. I have a friend; we will call her Églantine. Do not laugh, Désiré. My friend lives close by; she is, in fact, very well-to-do, and owns a café. I will go to her, and she will pack me a luncheon basket, and so we will be at the mercy of no landlord."

"Well, go," said Toto, "but do not be long."

"Half an hour is all I ask," replied the poet, rising in a great hurry and departing.

CHAPTER II.

FÊTE CHAMPÊTRE.

HE passed almost at a run down the Rue St. Honoré. A friend tried to stop him.

"I am busy," cried Gaillard; "do not detain me! *Mon Dieu!* I will pay you to-night! Meet me at eight at the Café de la Paix." Then, at a run, round the corner of the Rue Royale and into a large café just waking up: "Du Pont! Du Pont! Where is M. Du Pont?"

The proprietor, a large black-whiskered man in shirt-sleeves, appeared from the back premises, wiping his mouth with a serviette. This was Églantine.

"My dear Du Pont," cried Gaillard, "here am I nearly mad! M. le Prince has arranged a little picnic, and Sarony has forgotten to send the luncheon basket."

Du Pont flung up his hands as if the world had fallen in.

"Can you arrange a basket for three—cold fowl,

tongue, and some *pâté de foie gras*, also champagne?"

"How many for—three?" cried M. du Pont, holding up three fingers. "*Tenez!*" and away he rushed.

In ten minutes the basket arrived, borne by a waiter; it was a capable-looking basket, and seemed heavy.

"At least, we shall not starve," murmured Gaillard. "Charge it to M. le Prince, Du Pont. Adieu!" And he drove away in an open fly with the basket beside him, remembering, when it was too late, that he ought also to have ordered a box of cigars.

He met his companions in the Rue Mont Thabor; they had left the *crémerie*, and were walking up and down in the sun.

Then the trio, with the luncheon basket in their midst, drove off, and were deposited at the Gare du Nord, that dreary station with its multitudinous platforms and engines that do not whistle healthily, but toot mournfully with a suggestion of phantom horns.

Here in the hurry and hubbub the poet could express his ideas on the third-class tickets which Toto insisted on buying, without fear of Célestin overhearing his plaints.

"My dear Toto, do not do this disgraceful thing. Consider my position in the world, if you forget your own. Should anyone see me, *mon Dieu!* it will be all over Paris, and they will say my books are not selling. Already they are saying that the editions are being faked. I will go back, I will commit suicide——"

"Oh, rubbish! I'm going third. Stay behind if you like. *Ma foi!* see over there standing beside that woman with the plum-colored face! It's old De Nani, and he has seen us. Wait—wait for me, Célestin; I wish to speak to a friend. My dear Marquis," cried Toto, dragging the old man aside, "I am going on a little private business into the country. In fact, I am going with a lady and my friend Gaillard, but I do not want her to know my identity—you understand."

"*Parfaitement,*" replied the old beast, grinning under his paint and glancing at Célestin, and vowing in his own mind to do Toto an evil turn, if such a thing were possible.

For by a strange chance Struve's enemy, to whose house he had been driven drunk on the previous morning, was also his most deadly enemy. The Comte de la Fosse was this gentleman's name, and on descending in a flowered dressing gown on the previous morning to see what the hubbub was about, he had found M. le Marquis de Nani seated without his wig in the middle of the hall and singing ribald songs as he attempted to remove his boots. The Comte de la Fosse had ordered his enemy to be put to bed, and later in the day read him a pious lecture on the evils of drink and the disgrace he had brought on the old nobility. Toto was indirectly the cause of all this—directly, for all that old De Nani knew. Needless to say, he felt very bitter.

"And above all things," said Toto, "I don't want my mother to know."

"I understand," said De Nani. "I, too, am going into the country—to Chantilly."

"Good-by."

" *Au revoir*. But stay. Where shall I meet you again? Could I see you to-night?"

" Be at the Café de la Paix," said Gaillard, who had come up to see what was going on, and what this old blood-sucker was saying to his Toto, " and ask for M. Théodore Wolf. Anyone will show you him. He is a journalist with a black beard. I have made a rendezvous for eight with him. We will be there."

" Yes," said Toto, " be there at eight."

And De Nani left them, not for Chantilly, indeed, but to take a cab and drive to the Boulevard Haussmann and say to the Princesse de Cammora:

" Madame, something very strange is going on. Alas! it is not the fact of the young lady that alarms me, but, madame, he desired me not to mention her existence to you. Young men will be young men, but why this excessive secrecy? I have an intimate knowledge of the world, and I fear—— I do not like this M. Gaillard, either; he indulges most intemperately."

" Oh, Gaillard the poet," said the Princesse; " there is not much harm in him."

Still, she felt uneasy, and determined in her own mind to have an interview with Gaillard, and implore him to protect her precious Toto from the machinations of strange girls, and lead him into the right path—the path that led to Helen Powers.

"Why did you give that old fool a rendezvous at the Café de la Paix?" asked the Prince as the train whirled them along past green fields, on which Célestin's eyes were fixed with pathetic rapture.

"I did not give him a rendezvous," replied the poet, who had obtained Célestin's assent to his smoking one of Toto's cigarettes. "I shall not be there. Wolf will be there, and they will bore each other. Wolf is a dun, M. de Nani is a bore. I always appoint my duns and bores to meet each other at the Café de la Paix, the Café Américain, or the Grand Café. They dine together and speak ill of me whilst I am dining at Foyot's, or the Café Anglais, or the Maison Dorée. I have made the fortune of three cafés by the people I have sent there to wait for me. They all ask for each other, and sit at the same table and wait for me; then they dine, and as a rule drink too much champagne to assuage themselves——"

"*Mon Dieu*, Célestin!" cried Toto, seizing both her hands; "what is this? You are crying!"

"I have just remembered Dodor," sobbed Célestin. "I have left him shut up in my room, and, oh! should anyone open the door and leave it so, Mme. Liard's cat may kill him. *What* shall I do?"

"Why, the girl has a baby!" thought Gaillard in astonishment.

"Well, this is a nuisance!" said Toto in a voice of tribulation.

"How old is Dodor, mademoiselle?" asked the poet.

"He is two years and a little bit," wept Célestin.

"Ah, then be assured, mademoiselle, he is safe; cats never attack children of that age."

Toto made horrible faces at his companion.

"He is not a child, monsieur," murmured Dodor's mistress—"I often wish that he were; he is my lark, and Mme. Liard's cat may kill him."

Gaillard's eyes became filled with tears; a moment more, and he might have allowed himself the pleasure of weeping.

"Did you lock your door?" asked Toto.

"Why, yes, I did!" cried Célestin, brightening through her tears and putting her hand into the back pocket of her dress; "and the key—I have it. Oh, how relieved I feel! Still, I ought not to have forgotten him; he was a treasure given me by the good God to keep. Ah, monsieur," she said, turning to Gaillard, "you do not know how I love Dodor."

Gaillard's lachrymal works again began to threaten.

"Here we are," said Toto, and the train drew up at Montmorency, with the trees waving in the wind.

They came along the white road leading to the little town, a boy hired for half a franc carrying the basket, Gaillard threatening him with untold terrors if he dropped it and herding him with his crook-handled stick.

The blue sky was dotted here and there with little white clouds, like a sparse flock of white lambs tended by some invisible shepherd who had gone to sleep in the azure fields and left them to graze at their own sweet will. Beneath the sky and far away stretched the country, green as only April makes it, spread with apple blossom, the air filled with a sound one never hears in Paris—the hum of the wind in a million trees.

Célestin seemed tipsy. One can fancy a newly arrived angel in the fields of Paradise drunk with color and light. She dashed into hedgerows after wild flowers, and clapped her hands at butterflies, and cried out with happiness when she saw a lamb just like one of the lambs one sees in the Magazin du Louvre at Christmas time, but this one dancing round its mother in the middle of a field pied with daisies.

" She has gone mad," said Toto, delighted with the delight of his *protégée.*

" 'Tis the primitive woman breaking out," said Gaillard. " Proceed, Alphonse, and if you drop that basket I will flay you! Believe me, Désiré, every woman is a nymph at heart. I know several women who are devotees when in Paris, but in the country they become hamadryadic; 'tis the influence of the trees—they remember Pan.   Have you read my little brochure ' Pan in Paris '?   It appeared as a feuilleton in *Lucifer*, the journal of the Satanists.   I am not a Satanist; I despise the sect.   I went to their church once; Satan in person was to appear.   He did; the lights were lowered, but he did not frighten me, for I had heard him bleating in the vestry before he was brought on —it was a goat.   Besides it was very dull; I left in the middle of the sermon, and Satan smelt dreadfully.   I had to burn pastilles in my room for three days to help me to forget him."

They skirted the happy little town, and made for a part of the chestnut forest declared by Alphonse to be suitable for picnics.   Here, beneath the trees on the edge of the sunlight, the basket was deposited on the greensward, and Gaillard flung himself down to rest.

" I will leave you here," said Toto, " to get the things ready, and I will take Célestin to the hilltop to see the view."

" Leave me, then, your cigarette case," murmured Gaillard, his hat over his eyes, and his arms flung out on either side; "and do not be long, Désiré, for I am famished."

From the hill of Montmorency the whole world of April lay before them, in its midst Paris, the city of light, sixteen miles away, cream-colored and drab; Paris the noisy, silent amidst all that silent country stretching away in billows of tender green to the sky of pale and wonderful blue.

"Oh, *ciel!*" sighed Célestin, removing her gloves as she sat by Toto, and folding them carefully inside out and putting them in her pocket. "Can that be Paris, that little place? my thumb covers it when I hold it so. And, oh, the sky!—it seems to stretch to heaven. How happy the world is!"

"Do you find it happy?" asked Toto, tearing up wild violets and flinging them away to keep his hands employed.

"Yes," said Célestin, breathing the word out in a manner that made it a prayer of praise.

"But you are not rich—you are like me; and they say the rich see more of the pleasure of the world than we do. Tell me, would you like to be a great lady, one of those one sees in the Bois?"

"Oh, no!" said Célestin; "I would much rather be myself."

"But!" said Toto, tearing a daisy's head off, "imagine having money to spend, as much as one wanted."

"I have."

"Imagine having a carriage and horses."

"That would be nice; at least, I would sooner, I think, go in omnibuses—one would be very desolate all alone in a carriage. It is the people who make omnibuses so delightful; one wonders where they are going to and what they have in their baskets; and some read books, and one tries to imagine what they read of. And then the hats one sees! they make one want to laugh and weep. Sometimes they are not so bad, but sometimes they are frightful; often have I wished to say, ' Madame, let me retrim your hat; I will do it for love, and use my own thread,' but I have never dared."

"Well, imagine being able to ride in omnibuses all day long."

Célestin smiled, and looked away into the blue distance, as if she were watching an ethereal omnibus filled with her familiar angels.

" Well, you could do that all day if you were rich."

" I could not take Dodor."

Toto, the tempter, felt that she had him there, but he was not tempting her in the ordinary acceptation of the word.

" You love Dodor very much?" Her eyes swept round to him, and rested full upon his. " Tell me, Célestin: could you not love me a little too?"

When they got back to the picnic they found the cloth spread, the places laid, and the Perigord pie eaten; they had, in fact, been away over two hours, and the poet had not waited.

There was cold tongue, and part of a fowl and rolls and butter left, all of which Gaillard offered with effusion; he had expected a scolding for beginning without them, but he did not get it. Toto did not care, Célestin did not know; cold tongue or Perigord pie, it did not matter—they were in love. The poet smiled upon them like a father, and piled their plates, and gave them what was left of the champagne.

" Here's to Églantine! " said Toto, toasting the provider of the feast in a glass of Mumm, from which Célestin had taken a sip. " Has she brown eyes or blue? "

" Blue," said Gaillard. " Blue as the skies above Pentelicus."

" Well, tell her what I say, and give me a cigarette."

" There is only one left," replied the poet, as he hastily lit it.

CHAPTER III.

THEY returned to Paris at five, leaving the luncheon basket at the Montmorency Station.

"Églantine will send for it," said Gaillard.

At the Nord they took an open carriage driven by a cabman in a white beaver, and drawn by two white ponies. In this conveyance they tore down the Rue de Faubourg St. Denis, along the Boulevard Nouvelle, and down the Rue Richelieu. Toto sat beside Célestin; Gaillard on the front seat, his stick between his legs, chattered like a magpie, so delighted was he to find himself back in his dear Paris.

"Gaillard," cried Toto, when Célestin had been deposited at her own door, with a whispered word in her ear and a promise on her lips for a rendezvous on the morrow, "I am in love."

"*Ma foi!* I know."

"You don't; you know nothing of love, neither

you nor any of us. I don't know how many women have sworn that they love me; they do because
I am a Prince, because I am jewelry, good dinners,
and what not. (Boulevard Haussmann, you fool!
I have told you twice; and make those pigs of
horses travel faster—we are not a dung cart.)
Yes, I am all that, and they love me. De Nani, for
instance, is a pattern of truth and friendship, as we
know it. I have never seen our world before;
Célestin has lit it for me. My mother paints; good
God! my father painted; he wore stays."

"I, too, have worn stays," declared Gaillard—
"three years ago, when I was very young and foolish. I was then twenty-two. I discarded them
because they were such a trouble to lace. I have
even painted. What will you have? Youth must
expend itself; but believe me, Toto, our world is
not a bad world beneath the paint."

"I tell you it is a vile world."

"Well, perhaps it is, in parts. De Nani, for instance; beware of that old man, Toto. He is the
type of excess. An old man drunk and a drunken
old man are two different people. De Nani is a

habitual drunkard; I can read it in his eye. He is more dangerous than a cartful of women. Still, despite the fact of De Nani and a thousand like him, I have a childish faith in the world. I believe in humanity, or what I can see of it through the misery and mystery of life. I believe in flowers, I believe in trees. Have you read my ' Rose Worship'? *Mon Dieu!* what was that? Only a dog we have run over. Animals, too, are part of my creed. I am thinking of having a book of my belief published, with colored plates. It would be the bible of childhood. Flowers, beasts, birds, and insects would be as the four Apostles. I was saved from atheism by a butterfly. It flew into my rooms in the Rue de Turbigo one day last August. Everyone was at the seaside; I was alone in Paris. De Brie had refused to advance me the money for a trip to Normandy. You, Toto, were at Trouville. The day was sultry, and, to add to my pain, a barrel-organ played in the street outside. Mme. Plon brought me a letter. It was a draft from my sister for five hundred francs. As I cast my eyes over it, a white butterfly flew in through my window, thrice around the room, and out again. It was the voice of the Unseen, saying ' I am here.' Yes, I believe—I believe in your Célestin. She is all nature, and to be loved by such a woman is a benediction."

La Princesse de Cammora's carriage was at the door. She had just returned from shopping, and tea was being served to her in the drawing room.

Gaillard loved tea and Princesses,—even Princesses of fifty,—so he left Toto to go upstairs and change, whilst he found his way to the drawing room.

The Princesse was not alone—Pelisson was with her. He had come to find Toto. His head looked larger than ever; it seemed bursting with some great idea, and, true to his nature, he was making a noise. He was also making the Princesse laugh. The tears were in her eyes as Gaillard entered.

Gaillard sipped his tea whilst the journalist finished his story. It was about an actress. Then the Princesse drew Gaillard into a corner, leaving

Pelisson to look over a bundle of engravings till the coming of Toto.

"Oh, M. Gaillard," said the great lady in a motherly yet playful voice, "how naughty it is of you to lead my Toto astray! No, no, do not speak; it is not you I fear; but I have heard—no matter: a little bird told me. Now, this journey to the country. Who is she, M. Gaillard?"

"Madame, I swear to you——"

"Nay, nay, I do not want you to tell tales out of school; but you have been seen—the three of you—this morning at the Nord. Tell me, now—her name!"

"Madame, be assured, it was a most innocent freak. She is a most charming and innocent girl."

"Oh, this is dreadful!" murmured the Princesse. "M. Gaillard, I speak to you as a mother to a son. I do not mind Toto's Mimis and Lolottes,—one cannot keep a young man in a cage,—but I dread these innocent girls. I have seen, alas! so much of life. They come to the house and make disturbances; they have relations, old men from the country, who come and sit in one's hall till a *sergent-de-ville* is called. One need not be straitlaced, but one need not beat a tin pan over one's indiscretions. Besides, Toto is at a very critical age. I have a match at heart for him, a girl pure and beautiful as an angel. But she is an American, and they do not understand the little ways of young men. She is also a good match, even for Toto. So you see it is a mother's heart that speaks. I pray you tell me her name."

"Her name is Lu-lu," said Gaillard, Papillard coming to his aid.

"Lu-lu. Ah, that sets my heart at rest, M. Gaillard. There was never an innocent girl in Paris with that name."

"Madame," said the poet, "I think your perception is very clear. I would not disparage Mlle. Lu-lu's innocence; still, she has a habit of casting her eyes about, and speaks of ' larks.' "

"And tries to persuade poor Toto that she is an innocent. M. Gaillard, I have read your beautiful poems, and I know your mind, for I have seen it in your works. I have no fear of Toto whilst you are by; stay near him, M. Gaillard, watch over him."

" I will."

"And let me know how things go on. Hush! here he is."

Toto entered in evening dress, covered with a light overcoat.

" Hello, Pelisson! "

" M. Pelisson has called to take you to dine with him," said the Princesse. " He has some great journalistic feat to perform, and he wants your aid. Go, all of you, and be happy."

" I am bursting! " cried Pelisson, when they were in the street. " Toto, take my arm; Gaillard, give me yours. Cab! No, I must work my electricity off by walking. We will dine at the Café de la Paix. I met Wolf an hour ago; he told me he would be there."

" Stop," said Gaillard. " I do not want to go to the Café de la Paix."

" Why, Wolf told me you had a rendezvous with him."

" It was a *rendezvous de convenance*," said the

poet. "He is bothering me. Never knew a man to bother so over a paltry hundred francs."

"I will pay it," said Pelisson. "Come along. What's that you say: Old De Nani will be there—the Marquis? He'll do; I am in want of a cheap Marquis. Really, the gods are working. Hearken to Paris—it hums; I will make it roar. The Ministry is down. Have you not heard? Oafs! where have you been? Well, then, the time is coming; it only wants the men to bring it."

"The time has come for what?" asked Gaillard.

"For a general rooting out, all the rotten sticks into the fire. What will be the end of it?—who knows? The restoration of the Bourbons, I believe. The republic is a rotten hoarding, papered with Panama scrip. What's behind the hoarding? ah, ah, my children! wait and see. I am going to bring out a paper; everything is ready down to the printer's ink. I want from you a hundred thousand francs, Toto. I want your brains, Gaillard. Struve we will pull into it also. I have four other men; all the talent in Paris will be with me. It is to be a dull paper full of ideas.   It will lick the boots of the bourgeoisie, and wink behind it at the throne.   It will slaver, and stink, and shuffle along, but it will build barricades in the world of thought.   Gaillard, can you write an ode to a yard-stick?"

" I can write an ode to anything beautiful."

" What is more beautiful than a bourgeois?   He is the emblem of commerce."

" Looking at him in that light, he has his dim sort of beauty; besides, I would do anything to vex De Brie.   He pays one for one's work as if one were a butcher selling legs of mutton.   He reduces literature to the level of a trade.   He would be mad if he thought I were on the staff of another journal."

" He'll be madder when he sees my paper break out like the smallpox; but you must be dull."

" I would endeavor even to be dull," said Gail-lard, " to vex De Brie."

" But see here," said Toto.   " What is the use of another paper?   There are hundreds of papers."

"There is no paper like mine," said Pelisson. "Wait till you see it! it will begin with a grunt and end in a yell. *Ma foi!* yes. There are a hundred dull papers pretending to be clever, but there is no clever paper pretending to be dull. I am going to be respectable, and wear a scorpion's tail. I am going to give more business news than any other paper. M. Prudhomme will read me after dinner; and I will tickle him under the ribs, and then some day I will bite him behind, and make him jump from his easy-chair and pull things down. You will hear Paris crack. Here we are!"

They had reached the Café de la Paix; De Nani and Wolf were there already.

"For goodness' sake, Pelisson," said Gaillard, "give this wretched Wolf his hundred francs, or he will be making innuendoes all dinner-time! It is a way he has; he is most spiteful and has no reserve."

Wolf was a journalist, with a long black beard, a high forehead, and spectacles. His forte was interviewing. He entered one's house like a wolf, and swallowed one—house, wife, furniture, and all;

the backyard and the front garden were not beneath him. Then he vomited the remains into the columns of fifty papers, and went and devoured someone else. But he was a good-natured wolf, ready to lend to a friend in distress, but a terrible creditor, for, to use Gaillard's expression, he tortured one so.

Pelisson drew him aside and promised him payment, and then they dined, the journalist sketching out his plan between the courses to the delight of his listeners, excepting Toto.

The wretched Toto had no part in the scheme; they asked him for money to help them, but they did not invoke his brains. He felt the slight, but not severely; literature was not his path. He had no hankering after distinction as a journalist, so he agreed to supply the hundred thousand francs, if he could get them.

" I will give you bills at three months, and leave you to discount them. I am going to Corsica to shoot moufflon." And he touched Gaillard's foot under the table to remind him of Célestin and the attic in Bohemia.

"But," said De Nani, who had remained sober, for the gout was threatening, and, besides, there seemed to be a chance of money in all this, "what is the name of this journal to be?"

"*Pantin*," replied Pelisson. "I have sifted a hundred thousand names in my head during the last three days, and *Pantin* is the only one that stuck. It fits my idea like a glove; it has several meanings. It is like a stroke on a gong."

Pantin's health was drunk, then the conversation ran on, everyone talking except Toto, who was drinking.

Toto, to do him credit, rarely drank much; he drank to-night because the joy of the others depressed him. He could not share their excitement; he felt himself to be the drone in this hive; they were all famous in their way, these men, except De Nani. He and De Nani, the representatives of birth—what a pair! He drank double on account of De Nani.

They all rose from the table and trooped out, Pelisson's hand on everybody's shoulder, Wolf with his spectacles glittering in the gaslight, Gaillard gesticulating, De Nani sniggering, Toto smoking. They were going to Pelisson's rooms to formulate their plans on paper. Unhappy Toto, had he known the nasty trick *Pantin* was destined to play him!

CHAPTER IV.

RECEIPT FOR STUFFING A MARQUIS.

SOME days later Gaillard was lying in bed. It was noon, and the blinds of his room were down. Toto burst in.

"Go away, Toto," said the poet in a feeble voice. "I am dying."

"What are you dying of?"

"Misery," murmured Gaillard, turning his face to the wall.

Toto pulled up the blind.

"Never mind the misery. Get up and come out; I want you. What's the matter?"

"The world; it comes upon me like this sometimes, the horror of the whole thing. Besides, someone stole all my money last night. Where is God? I do not know. Go away, and leave me to myself."

"You haven't taken poison or anything, have you?"

" No—not yet."

" Well, get up, and I will give you some money, and we will go and have *déjeuner*."

Gaillard moved uneasily.

" Do be quick, or I will go without you."

The poet rose rapidly, and began to dress.

" I have seen Célestin," said Toto, standing by the window, and looking out on the street.

" Ah, that charming Célestin! " sighed Gaillard, putting on his trousers with a weary air.

" And I have taken an atelier in the Rue de Perpignan. I spent the whole afternoon yesterday hunting for that fool Fanfoullard; no one knew of such a person, but I found very nice rooms."

" Fanfoullard has left Paris—gone to Nimes. But, Toto, what is this you tell me? Are you really going to start on this crusade—become a painter? "

" I am a painter."

" I mean, live in this dreadful way? Toto, I predict that there will be great trouble. Your mother is very anxious; she is anxious for you to make a good match."

" That's all right."

" How all right? " asked Gaillard, scratching his head.

" I saw the American girl yesterday, and told her what I was going to do. She is going to keep my mother quiet; she fell in with the idea at once. She is the only person who understands me."

" Did you tell her of Célestin? "

" No, of course I did not; I am not that sort of person. I never talk of one woman before another. Go on dressing."

" And I suppose you will end by marrying the beautiful American, when you are famous? "

" I will never marry anyone but Célestin. She is the only woman I have ever loved."

" But, *mon Dieu!* you are not going to marry her? "

" No; I would if she wanted to, but she doesn't. A priest mumbling over us will not make us love each other any more. Don't put on that awful green necktie, for goodness' sake; take that plaid one, it looks better."

" And you are going to start your *ménage* to-morrow?" asked Gaillard, putting on the desired necktie carefully before the glass.

"Yes, and that is what I am going to start on."

He held out three bank-notes for a thousand francs each.

"It won't last you a month."

"It will have to last me a year."

"Toto, are you serious?"

"What the deuce!" blazed out Toto. "Every-one asks me that when I want to do anything that is not foolish. When I took to painting first, that fool De Harnac raised his stupid eyebrows and said: 'Toto, are you serious?' When I told Helen Powers yesterday, the first thing she said was, 'Toto, are you serious?' And now you. Am I a buffoon? And stop calling me by that odious name: I am Toto no longer—I am Désiré. Are you dressed? Let us go, then."

"But I do not know what will become of me," said Gaillard, as they descended the stairs. "What will become of me, all alone in Paris, without you? I shall be bored; I shall die of yawning."

"You can come over every day and see us."

" It is so far."

" You can take an omnibus."

" A what? An omnibus! I!"

" They are good enough for Célestin; they are good enough for me; but see here, Gaillard: above all things, you must not tell anyone what I am going to do or where I am going. I am going to amuse myself. Well, what does it matter to people whether I am amusing myself by shooting in Corsica or by painting in the Rue de Perpignan? "

" I will be mute as a fish."

" I have joined a studio—Melmenotte's. I want to do a lot at the nude. I will sell my studies as I go on. A student there told me it was quite easy to live by pot-boiling, but I am going to have a great work in hand. How can a man work leading the life we lead? The other morning, just as I was settling down to a picture, Valfray came and dragged me off to that cock-fight at Chantilly. I got a blouse yesterday for six francs. Come in here, I want to see Pelisson; he is sure to be here at this hour."

They entered a café on the Boulevard des Capucines, and there sure enough sat Pelisson; he had finished his *déjeuner* and was reading letters.

" How's *Pantin?* " asked Gaillard.

" Blooming, or going to bloom. I am besieged with firms who want to advertise."

" Have you fixed on your editor? "

" De Nani."

" What! " asked Gaillard in a horrified voice. " That drunken old wretch! "

" Pah! he is only the figurehead. I am the editor; no one knows him, that is the charm. He has been lying *perdu* at Auteuil for half a century, and now I have got him, he is only a skin; I am going to stuff him—stuff him with Pelisson. Already people are asking who is this Marquis de Nani, and people are answering he is the editor of the new journal that is going to be, *Pantin*, the wittiest man in Paris, and discovered by Pelisson. I am circulating *bonmots* of De Nani's; they are mine, but nobody knows that. In a week's time everyone will be talking of De Nani, this Marquis who is a genius; everyone will be craving to see him. You know Paris. The old fool is wise enough to dodge round corners, for he knows his own stupidity; should anyone find it out, they will put it down to his cleverness. Wolf is publishing an interview with him written by me. Oh, yes! *Pantin* will be a success, and you will have your hundred thousand francs back, Toto, and a hundred thousand on top of it."

" You got the bills discounted? "

" Oh, yes."

" What is this I hear about a new journal? " asked Struve, who had come in unobserved, slipping into a chair beside Pelisson.

The newspaper man explained whilst Toto and Gaillard breakfasted.

" And Toto pays for all this? "

" He has good security; besides, he only pays a third. I have two hundred thousand francs from a little syndicate, and the promise of five hundred thousand if the thing takes. Toto has a lien on the advertisements; he is perfectly safe."

" What's De Nani's salary? "

" I give him a dinner every day and ten francs."

" Have you a cash-box? "

" Why? "

" Keep it locked.   Pelisson, you are a fool."

" Why? "

" To have let that old goat into your affair."

" You wait and see."

" I will."

" You are not going? "

" I am."

" But see here: I want a man to do the art criticism."

" You'll find lots."   And Struve vanished.

" He always throws cold water on everything," said Toto, remembering the advice about the coffee mill.

" He's a critic," said Gaillard.

" He's a clever man," said Pelisson, knitting his brows an instant; " but he's wrong here."

" Oh, the middle of the day! " cried Toto in a voice of tragedy as he took the poet's arm half an hour later and lounged out of the café.   " What a frightful institution it is!   I would like to be born into a world where the days had no middles."

" You are right; it is a most inartistic flaw in the scheme of things.   The night has no such blunder; that is why I love it.   The night always reminds me of the exquisite masterpiece of some forgotten painter in the gallery of some bourgeois millionaire. Every twelve hours we slip into the exquisite poem of darkness, and then out again into this villainous prose.   Pah! if I had the key of the meter that feeds our great chandelier, men would have a three-hours' day; it is quite long enough."

" Quite.   I am going to look at my new rooms; will you come?   We will take a cab."

They drove to the Rue de Perpignan; it was a long street situated in what remains of the Latin Quarter.   Gaillard shivered at the everyday appearance of the place.   He had never been in it before; the name, floating loose in his head, had attached itself to the name of Fanfoullard; he wished now that he had never imagined the fan-painter.

" It is a great way from everywhere, do you not think, Désiré?   Why put the Seine between one's self and civilization?   One can hide one's self just as easily a hundred yards from the Rue St. Honoré as a hundred miles."

Toto made no answer, but led the way upstairs.

The atelier was certainly large enough; men were at work settling the stove; another man was mending the top light. The place was almost studiously bare; a tulip in the bud in a red-tile pot stood on a table; an old guitar hung on the wall; there was a throne and drapery, an easel, or, at least, three. Some of these things had belonged to the last tenant. The tulip in the pot had, however, only just arrived. It suited the surroundings, which were those of an ordinary atelier; yet there was something about the place suggestive of a scene in a theater. Perhaps it was the guitar. But one felt the hand of Henri Murger over it all.

"This," said Toto, touching a nail in the wall, "is for Dodor's cage."

Gaillard's heel struck against the handle of a little frying-pan that protruded from a bundle.

"We will have our meals sent in, but it is useful sometimes to be able to cook at home—sausages and things. You must come and teach us how to make coffee."

Gaillard poked his nose into an adjoining room; it was a bedroom. He observed that the washing-jug was cracked.

"Well," said Toto, "what do you think of it all?"

"I envy you."

CHAPTER V.

ANGÉLIQUE.

"I ENVY you," said Gaillard as they returned to civilization; "I envy you because you are young, rich, and a Prince. I do not envy you for these things, but rather for the enjoyment they can give you. To be twenty-two, poor, and in love—what can be better than that? You are twenty-two, and in love, and you are so rich that you can allow yourself the luxury of being poor. What a change for you, and how you will taste it all! Poverty falls to the poor; they have it every day, but they do not enjoy it. It is like the old women who sell sugar-plums; they do not eat their own wares. But with you it will be different; you will bring an unsated palate. Your present, contrasted with your past, will be as a naked man standing against a background of old-gold brocade. Extraordinary being to have found out a new pleasure in this

jaded age, and that pleasure lying unnoticed before
the eyes of all men.   Look at that beggar man—
are not his clothes the color of withered leaves?   I
have seen greens in old coats that no painter has
ever seized.   You would never guess my deep acquaintance with the ways of the poor, but I have
been thrown in their way.   Toto, I have a girl-
friend."

" Better say a dozen."

" I know girls pursue me, but I cast them off.
Angélique is not of the common order."

" Who is Angélique, for goodness' sake? "

" She is the only woman I love."

" I have heard you say that a dozen times about
a dozen women."

" I was only pretending; in this world one hides
one's pearls and wears one's glass beads.   Angélique is very poor; she is a *pompon* maker."

" What's a *pompon?* "

" A *pompon* is a thing women wear in their hats
—a little fluffy feather, an absurdity, but it supports Angélique.   In this world, Toto, some fate
ordains that men live on each other's absurdities.

Absurdity is to men as grass to cattle, air to life. Could you place a great cupping-glass over Paris, and, with an air-pump, remove all its absurdity, the place would fall to pieces; ten thousand men would starve; the journals would wither like autumn leaves; Struve, Pelisson, De Brie, and a thousand others would vanish; women would no longer wear *pompons* in their hats, and poor little Angélique would die from want of folly in others. Angélique has a lame brother who lives at Villers Cotterets; he is a great trial to us—an incessant drain. You often laugh at me for my expenses; the fact is, Toto, I am always being tapped, like a person with the dropsy. The affection between this brother and sister is a poem; I weep my money away over it. Now you are casting in your lot with art, Angélique rises up in my mind, and I hear her say " What will become of me? " I will not hide it from you that you have, through me, been the mainstay of an unfortunate man. Angélique knows it. Well, I want you to leave in my hands a certain provision for these people before you cut yourself off from your resources."

" I'll give you some money to-morrow; I want you to come and see me started."

" Where shall I call for you? "

" At the Boulevard Haussmann."

" In the morning? "

" Yes, and be sure that you say nothing of all this; I want no one to know what I am doing."

" But your mother? "

" She does not care so long as the American does not know."

" Do not yawn so, Toto."

" I can't help it; it's the thought of my mother, and old De Nani, and all the lot.　Do you know, some day or another I would have cut my throat if I had not met Célestin; she was like a breath of air—she understands me because she loves me. Oh, I'm so sick of women *grinning* at me; Célestin is the only woman I have ever seen smile.　Mlle. Powers is a nice girl; she means what she says, but she always talks to me as if I were her grandchild, and she calls me Toto.　Won't it be a joke when my mother finds out that I have given old Pelisson -

a hundred thousand francs! I am fond of Pelisson, he's the best of the lot; I'd do anything for him."

" Pelisson has his limitations," said Gaillard, and Toto yawned again.

CHAPTER VI.

THE DEPARTURE.

GAILLARD, who was somewhat of a philosopher, had once divided sorrow under two heads—the sorrows of life and the sorrows of art. He reckoned the necessity of getting up early chief amidst the mundane sorrows, and accepted it in a grumbling spirit; but this morning he did not grumble. He dressed rapidly and sadly, and departed for the Boulevard Haussmann, refusing the coffee and roll and butter offered to him by Mme. Plon.

"I cannot eat," said Gaillard. "I am deeply disturbed."

He found Toto dressed and in his atelier. He was looking at Sisera and Jael. Jael had the air and aspect of a stout housemaid nailing carpets down with energy.

"How could I have painted that beast?" asked Toto. "She is all flesh, she is an animal, she is like a bull-fighter in a skirt. Imagine a woman like that, and then imagine Célestin."

"Are you going to remove these canvases to your new atelier? "

" *Mon Dieu,* no! I will remove nothing that reminds me of this place. I tell you what: I will make you a present of this picture. You can have the water-nymph too."

" Thanks," said Gaillard in an unenthusiastic voice. " I will not remove them at present; they would remind me too much of all the pleasant times that are gone. I feel very depressed this morning, Toto—I mean Désiré; one cannot get out of old habits in a hurry without shivering."

He looked out of a side window and away over the roofs of Paris. The morning was sitting on the roofs pelting the city with roses; the city grumbled, Gaillard sighed.

" Oh, the good times, how they pass! Do you remember, Désiré, the night you won a thousand napoleons at the Grand Club? It is only a month ago, yet it seems a year."

" The night we tied the two cats by the tail and

hung them from a lamp-post? Where did De Mirecourt get those cats? He suddenly appeared with them. Do you remember the *sergent-de-ville* who tried to get them down?"

"I had forgotten the incident of the cats. I remember it dimly, now—one was a tortoise-shell. Yes, those were pleasant times. Désiré, it is not too late to go back to them; consider your position well before you take this step."

"Come," said Toto, "I am going."

"But have you said good-by to Mme. la Princesse?"

"She would never forgive me for waking her at this hour."

"*Mon Dieu!* but you have no luggage."

"I have a bag in the hall below."

"Ah, *mon Dieu!* I hope this is all for the best. So you are going with only a bag? Désiré, have you forgotten Angélique?"

"I have three thousand francs in an envelope— it will keep you going. Do try and make it do for six months. Look at me; I have only three thousand for a year."

"I will try. Ah, *mon Dieu!* I wish I had never seen this day; my heart is heavy. Thanks, I will not open the envelope till I meet Angélique; we will open it together. We are like two children sitting at a feast and pulling crackers; each day is like a cracker tied with dawn-colored ribbon. Sometimes Angélique weeps at the contents of these crackers, sometimes she laughs and claps her hands; she will clap her hands to-day. Come, let us go and follow our fates."

"This is my luggage," said Toto, picking up a huge Gladstone bag in the hall.

Gaillard opened the hall door, and they passed out into the bright morning. The clock of St. Augustin was striking eight; the sparrows were fighting in the sunshine; the earth seemed teeming with life and light and happiness.

"How good it all is!" said Toto, as they drove over the Seine. He was echoing Célestin's eternal sentiment without knowing it. "What a lovely world it is, and how little we see of it! We snore in our beds during the best part of the day, and live the rest of our time by lamplight."

" The world," said Gaillard, " always reminds me of a poem written by a shopkeeper to advertise his stale wares, unpunctuated and filled with printer's errors; that is why we read it by a dim light. It ought to have been burnt; it was unfortunately published and given to us to read. No one can make out what it is driving at; we have been spelling at it now a million years; we began when we were apes, and we will end, perhaps, when we are donkeys. I am sick of it; I would jump into the Seine, only that such an act would delight De Brie."

The cab stopped at the doorway of Célestin's house, and the concierge, Mme. Liard, greeted Toto effusively. Her heart was touched by the youth of the lovers and the fact of Toto being an artist; that he should take Célestin under his protection seemed to her as natural as the mating of sparrows, and a piece of very good fortune for Célestin.

Her trunk stood in the passage, and on the trunk the parrot cage, covered with green baize. From the cage came the occasional flirting sound of wings, the occasional tinkle of the swinging ring—sounds that bespoke uneasiness in the mind of Dodor.

Then Célestin came down the steep stairs, blushing, and Gaillard had to admit that, even if the world were an ill-written poem, it had at least some very beautiful passages; for Célestin had made for herself a hat which was an amorous dream, and a girl friend, some lower Célestin of the Rue St. Honoré, had, in a fit of sentiment, confected for her a gown such as an angel in half-mourning need not have been ashamed of. Toto had bought her a new pair of shoes, and she wore openwork stockings. Toto kissed her before everyone; this was their only marriage service.

" It makes me feel young again! " cried Mme. Liard as she carried the parrot cage out, whilst the driver carried the trunk. " And I will come and see you in your new home; and oh, monsieur,"—to Gaillard,—" she ought to be careful, for her chest is not what it should be; it was what killed her mother."

" I will see that she wears a muffler," replied

Gaillard, whilst Célestin got into the carriage, weeping from grief and happiness, and kissing her hand to Mme. Liard.

Then the vehicle drove away, Gaillard on the front seat, the lovers facing him, and Dodor's cage beside the coachman.

Part III.

CHAPTER I.

GARNIER.

THE *rapin* of Paris is the sparrow of the artistic temple, but he is much more besides. For one thing, he is sometimes an eagle in disguise. He laughs as he paints, and plays dominoes with fantastic gravity. He is generally ugly, but he loves Beauty, and draws her in all postures, even immodest ones. Sometimes he becomes literary, and publishes a journal the size of a prayer-book, in which he has written nonsense and which lives for three months. In this way, I suppose, he takes a vague sort of revenge for all the nonsense that has been written about him.

I do not think you will find in Europe a more foul-minded person than the *rapin*, or a more joyous, or a more lovable, or a more pitiable. And though he is certainly the most consequential creature in the world, he is the greatest knocker-down of pedestals. Delacroix declared he could smell corruption in the air of Paris. I think he must have smelt the *rapin.* Yet out of this dung spring the fairest flowers of art.

Toto, forsaking his world for a space, had cast in his lot with this creation, and Célestin, like an angel made blind by love, followed him. Dodor had no voice in the matter, yet he endeavored to put it in as he swung in his cage from the nail in the wall.

"Oh!" sighed Célestin next morning as she sat beside Toto on the couch opposite the stove. "Am I on earth still, or can it be that we are in heaven?"

In one day she had become a woman without ceasing to be an angel, and Dodor sang as if to assure her of the fact, whilst Toto kissed her, and a beam of sun through the top light touched the tulip.

That was their morning, spent amidst the great flowers of the chintz-covered couch, whilst time passed over them like a butterfly with blue wings, and Paris grumbled through the top light like a jealous monster.

In the afternoon Toto, in his blouse, settled his painting things and rearranged drapery, whilst his companion, whose fingers could not be still, turned the morning, gone now forever, into a hat. She murmured to the hat as she made it, telling it of her happiness—a most adorable soliloquy lost to the world forever, for Toto was too busy to note it down. Then, when the structure was finished, she held it out on her finger-tip for admiration. It blushed there as if ashamed of its beauty and happiness. And Toto said " It is beautiful," in an abstracted voice, for he was hunting for a palette-knife.

They dined at a little restaurant near the Palais Bourbon, and spent their evening at the Porte St. Martin Theater, where a bloody drama was enacted, which caused Célestin to weep deliciously and shiver.

This was their honeymoon, for next day work began in earnest, and Toto started for Melmenotte's studio, a large bleak room filled with can-

vases and diligent students, a naked woman, large
and solid and sitting on a throne, in their midst.

They hazed him at first, but he did not lose his
temper, so they left him alone; besides, he showed
no talent, therefore created no envy, hatred, or
malice.

But Garnier, the man who worked on his right,
took an interest in him just, perhaps, because the
others voted him uninteresting and his work hope-
less. It was Garnier's way; he was a friend of failures, and took an interest in the forlorn. Sparrows, stray cats, or people like Toto appealed to
him strangely.

He was an immense fellow, with Southern blood
in his veins and hopes of humanity, and his secret
ambition in life was to be a politician and set the
world to rights. Nature, however, the sworn foe
of secret ambitions, had placed all his talents in his
eyes and fingers, insisting that this wayward child
should be no politician, but a divine artist.

He had a great reputation as a scamp. He swore
terrifically, and could out-talk a washerwoman.
He was always borrowing, and spending, and lend-

ing, and giving, and he boasted that he kept a mistress.   No one ever saw her; he kept her jealously hid, for she was eighty.   He had, in fact, met her one day on one of the bridges crossing the Seine, and pensioned her forthwith because she reminded him of his mother, whom he had never beheld.

He was a love-child, it seems, and certainly a most terrible mixture as far as mind and morals were concerned, for his ideals were always very high, and his ideas often very low, and his language very often pornographic.   To complete himself, he always stank of garlic, and his pockets were generally stuffed with cheap cigarettes and sweets, which he dispensed open-handed to his friends.

" Thanks," said Toto, taking a cigarette from a dozen held out by Garnier.

It was the third morning of his attendance at the studio, and he was feeling depressed; he was also putting away his things, for it was Saturday, and work stopped at twelve.

" I," said Garnier, " am going to enjoy myself, but the question is, How?   Shall I go home and go to bed and read Eugène Sue, or shall I go to

the Tobacco-Pot and play dominoes?   Jolly, have
you any money?"

"None," answered a lank-haired and evil-faced
youth, darting out of the room, and clattering away
down the stairs after the others.

"I have," said Toto.

"How much?" inquired Garnier, with the air of
a judge.

"Ten francs."

"That settles it.   We will go to the Tobacco-
Pot. Ten francs, and this is Saturday! *Mon
Dieu*, what a Rothschild you must be!   Where did
you get your money from?"

"My father."

"What is he?"

"He keeps a shop."

"Happy for you.   You can paint away, and the
old bird feeds you.   Oh, I should like a shop—a
little shop, where I would sell sweets and cigarettes,
and live in my shirt-sleeves, and read the *Ami du
Peuple* and kick my heels."

"What do you think of my work?" asked Toto,
glancing at the mediocre drawing upon his canvas.

" It's capital," said Garnier, his mind running on his little shop, where children would toddle in with their sou for sugar-sticks, and old women totter in for hap'orths of snuff: for, though Garnier loved all humanity, he perhaps loved the two extremes, childhood and old age, most.

" What made Melmenotte turn up his nose at it the way he did this morning when he came round? "

" He never praises anyone—he's a fossil. Come, let us be off to the Tobacco-Pot. Annette will be here in a moment to clear up."

" Come home with me and have some *déjeuner;* that will be better than the Tobacco Pot," said Toto, as they went down the stairs.

" To your father's place? "

" Oh, no; my atelier—Rue de Perpignan. I will introduce you to my—wife."

" *You* married! " cried Garnier, stopping in astonishment, and clutching Toto's arm. " Why, you are scarcely out of the egg! "

" I am twenty-two."

" *Mon Dieu!* well, why not? it is the happiest life.

Oh, I should like to have a wife and twelve little children all three years old. That is the age of all others; they talk like birds, and sentences from heaven slip into their conversation; and tumble on their noses, and pull one's beard. I have always seen myself as I ought to be some day, with a big stomach, sitting in an armchair, the children pulling my watch-chain, and mamma plying her needle, whilst the cat purred on the hearth: and here are you, three years younger than I am, and you have it all. What an eye the Germans have for children! how they draw them! *Mon Dieu!* I can almost forgive them Sédan for the sake of those adorable little Fritzes and Gretchens one sees in their funny little books."

They reached the Rue de Perpignan at last, and found *déjeuner* waiting. There was a little salad, some stewed beef, and a bottle of white wine, also some fruit on a plate.

As Toto and Célestin embraced, Garnier looked around him with a sigh. His room was an attic, yet I doubt if he would have exchanged his attic, where he lay abed on Sunday reading the " Mys-

teries of Paris" and imagining himself Prince Rudolph, and of a week-day night reading the *Intransigèant* by the light of a tallow candle and imagining himself Henri Rochefort, for this atelier, even
were Célestin thrown in—at least, at present.

Not that he undervalued Célestin, even at the
first glance; far from it. The great, noisy Garnier
was silent and quelled for quite ten minutes. He
had never met Célestin before amidst all the women
he had met, and he seemed undecided for a while as
to whether an angel or a child was dispensing the
cold stewed beef and the salad. Then he made up
his mind, evidently, that it was a child, and began
to play with her. He told stories, really droll little
stories, that a child or a man might laugh over, and
stainless as the white roads of Provence. And he
mimicked old men and women without malice, and
in such a way that Célestin wept from laughing.

After *déjeuner* he taught his hostess how to make
cat's cradles, and Dodor's history was told to him
whilst he sat on the couch and nursed his knee and
smoked his villainous cigarettes of Caporal.

The guitar was taken down from the wall, and he

played *café-chantant* songs, things with the ghost of an air moving in a whirl of sound, and sang the " Girls of Avignon " with tears in his eyes, that seemed to behold the whirl of the farandole, the white road to Arles, the moonlight, the fireflies, and the orange trees shivering in the mistral.

Altogether it was a most enjoyable afternoon, and the excitement and laughter left Célestin quite spent.   A fit of coughing seized her when the time came for them to go out to dinner, and she declared that she must lie down.   So she lay down on her bed, and Toto covered her up with a shawl, and gave her one of the lozenges Mme. Liard had placed in her trunk to suck.

Then he went out with Garnier, and they dined at a little café for two francs each, wine included.

" I found this little café only three months ago," said Garnier.   " It is a wizard café.   I dine here as often as I can, for some day I expect to find it vanished.   Those whom the gods love die young, and I am sure the gods must love this little café.   I cannot tell how they give one such a dinner for two francs, including a bottle of Maconolais.   That hare soup was a miracle. I suspect the miracle to be cats. But no matter; the taste was right. I save up on week-days, and dine here on Sundays."

" How long have you been working at art? "

" Five years."

Toto felt rather aghast.

" Have you been working at Melmenotte's atelier all that time? "

" Oh, no; for the last two years I have been in his private studio; it is being altered just now, so I just come to herd with the rest to keep my hand in. I must be doing something."

" Have you exhibited yet? "

" No; Melmenotte will not let me. I am to next year; I shall have a picture in the Salon next year."

" How sure he is of himself! " thought Toto. " And how dull he must be to have worked five ea s without exhibiting! " Then to Garnier: " One of the fellows told me one could live by selling pot-boilers."

" Yes; one could live by house-painting, for the matter of that. Who was it told you? "

"That young fellow with the long hair—Jolly you called him, I think."

"He is an awful wretch, that man, but a fine artist. Beware of him; do not ask him to your home. I never speak bad of people; but Jolly is not a person: he is a genius who will die in a jail or a lunatic asylum. I've told him so often. It would not do for him to make the acquaintance of Mlle. Célestin."

Garnier gave a little sigh as he ate a lark on toast, which he declared he suspected of being a rat. He seemed thinking a great deal of Célestin. The talk wandered over a number of topics, but somehow always back to or near Célestin.

Then Toto paid the score, and produced so much money that Garnier borrowed a napoleon in as natural a manner as that of a bee taking a suck at a flower. He then, as they walked away smoking Trabucos, bought a copy of the *Intransigèant,* and wandered home to read it, reminding Toto as they parted to give his regards to Célestin.

CHAPTER II.

A WEEK passed, making in all ten days of the new life, and still the novelty of it had not palled; but five hundred francs of the three thousand were gone. Where were they gone to? Toto scratched his head. Célestin helped him in his accounts, casting her beautiful eyes up as if for her angels to help her; but they were very bad mathematicians, these angels, though perfect milliners.

Garnier, in his big way, had declared to the studio that Toto was the best of good fellows when one got to know him. Jolly had pricked his ears at this, and instantly borrowed twenty-five francs from the new man, to send to his brother in the country; several others had done likewise, but this only accounted for eighty francs or so. True, they had paid the restaurateur and the washwoman; and they had gone the Sunday before to the Buttes Chaumont, so they finished making up their accounts with a kiss, and declared they must be more careful in the future.

"I will sell some hats," said Célestin, "and, oh, I know: we will get a money-box. It is wonderful, a money-box. Dodor has quite a fortune since I started his. Money seems to grow in a money-box. Kiss me again, Désiré."

Sometimes Toto thought of the world he had left. What were they all doing? Sometimes he felt slightly uneasy at the great absence of Gaillard. The poet had promised to call in three or four days, and, lo! ten had passed. His friends thought him in Corsica, but what was his mother doing? He had entered into a compromise with her not to bother him, and Helen Powers had promised to use her influence that he might be left alone to follow his art. Still, he felt nervous that some day Mme. la Princesse might break her word and arrive on the scene. She did not know his address, it is true; but, still, she had a way of finding things out.

He had worked fairly hard during these ten days, all things considered, and Garnier had dropped in to visit them now and then, bringing presents of sweets for Célestin.

Toto in the eyes of Garnier seemed a very enviable person. His father had a shop, and all shop-keepers, in the eyes of Garnier, were desperately rich; besides, the little *ménage* in the Rue de Per-pignan did his heart good. The lovers seemed so young and innocent, their way of life so ideal, and their conversation so charming, especially Célestin's.

It was on the twelfth day that Gaillard burst in upon them. Celestin was out marketing, Toto was at home smoking cigarettes, for it was the day Melmenotte came round,—that is to say, Saturday, —and Toto had taken a dislike to the great painter: he was not a gentleman.

Gaillard had a debauched air, and three books under his arm; and Toto, who had somehow been very much in the blues, felt an unholy joy at the sight of the poet.

" *Pantin* is out," said Gaillard, collapsing into a chair and flinging all his books on the floor. He produced a heavy and respectable-looking journal from his back pocket and cast it to the painter.

Toto scarcely glanced at it.

" Where have you been all this time? "

" Ah, my God! you may well ask me that. I have been at the beck and call of Pelisson. It is cruel; I have done all the work, and De Nani is getting all the praise; everyone is talking of De Nani— his jokes, his witticisms, his women, his wealth. And the old fool has not three ideas in his head, nor three sous in his pocket; no woman would look at him twice, and he never made a *bonmot* in his life. My ' Fall of the Damned ' came out the day before yesterday; no one is speaking of it, everyone is talking of De Nani. He has killed my little book, he and *Pantin.* It is all Pelisson's fault. He is only using De Nani as an advertisement. Struve was right: this old man is a goat; he smells like one, faugh! and he paints his face. Struve is the only man of sense of the lot. I always said so. Give me an absinthe, Toto; my nerves are gone."

" But how did Pelisson get his paper out so quickly? " asked Toto, helping the poet to a glass of vermouth, and feeling a dim sort of pleasure at his trouble.

"He has been working like a mole for months. You know the *Trumpet;* it came to grief last month; he has bought the plant and offices for a song. They are situated near the offices of the *Figaro* in the Rue Drouot. Oh, you should see that villain of a De Nani; he has bought a white hat, or got it on credit. He dines every day with Pelisson in a *cabinet particulier* at the Anglaise. No one is admitted, for fear they would find out the fraud, and the fact that he has no brains. Pelisson makes him drunk and sends him off in a cab to Auteuil, and then goes about telling people all the quaint things he has said. He is absorbing all Pelisson's money. Pierre has never a sou now to lend to a friend, and one can't dine with him, for he dines alone with De Nani. Conceive my feelings: this old beast has killed my book, cut off my supplies, and to crown all, wherever I go I hear nothing but De Nani, De Nani, De Nani! My God, I will go mad! Give me another vermouth."

"What are those books?" asked Toto, handing the glass.

"Those? They are insult added to an injury— books for review, and such books! See here Fourrier's 'Social Economy'; I am to write a trenchant quarter-column review of it, and abuse it, for that will please the bourgeoisie. I know nothing of social economy, so how can I abuse it? I could praise it, for then Fourrier, whoever he is, would not reply; besides, one can praise a book with one's eyes shut—bah! See here, a brochure on the American sugar trust. *Mon Dieu!* does Pelisson take me for a grocer? And here, again, a drama called 'Henri Quatre,' by some silly beast called Chauveau; all the lines limp, it is written in five-footed hexameters; and I am to praise it with discretion. With discretion, mind you! I wrote him a little poem for his abominable *Pantin;* it was called 'Carmine-Rouge.' You know I scarcely ever touch color in poetry; but I made an exception for once. He would not publish it; it was indecent, forsooth, and would bring the blush to the cheek of the bourgeoisie. Between the bourgeoisie on one hand and De Nani on the other, I feel as if I were in a terrible nightmare."

" Have you heard anyone speak of me? "

" No one; they think you are in Corsica. But I have seen Mme. la Princesse; she sent for me to inquire after your health, and how you were progressing."

" And you said——"

" Oh, I said ' Admirably '; it was the best thing to say. I promised to call again and inform her of your progress; she entreated me to implore you not to discard your woolen vests. There was also a message about an overcoat, which I have forgotten; it was either to wear one or not wear one, but I cannot tell which: you know a mother's ways. Toto, I feel hungry; have you anything to eat in this atelier of yours? "

Toto got together some bread and butter, half a cold tongue, and a bottle of wine. Gaillard turned up his nose at the feast provided for him, but began to eat.

" Toto, how much longer are you going to remain in this wretched Rue de Perpignan? Everywhere I go the cry is ' Where is Toto?' or ' When will Toto be back?'"

"Why, you said a moment ago nobody asked for me."

"Neither do they, but they speak of you, nevertheless; they do not ask for you because they imagine you in Corsica, but they mourn your absence."

"Oh, bother them—let them mourn!" said Toto in a gruff voice, chewing his cigarette in an irritable manner.

"And how is Art going on?" asked Gaillard, casting his eyes about as if he were looking for her.

"All right; don't bother me. I'm sick of talking art; tell me, How is Struve?"

"Struve is very well, though he declares that De Nani makes him sick."

He finished the wine in the bottle, and proceeded to the question of a loan.

"But," said Toto in horror, "you surely have not spent all that three thousand francs I gave you?"

Gaillard laughed harshly.

"Do I ever spend money? I spend my life paying it out, it seems to me; but how much do I spend on myself, how much have I for pleasure? Not a denier. I assure you, Toto, if I have three francs in my pocket people seem to smell it. No sooner had I got home the other day than Mme. Plon appeared with a bill, which I had imagined paid. Then Brevoart attached me for seven hundred and fifty. It was my fault for dealing with a German tailor; he got an order against me, and would have attached my royalties had I not paid. People think you are in Corsica, and so they make raids on me—then there is Angélique."

"But, see here: I am very hard up myself. You know I determined to do on three thousand; well, I have spent over five hundred in a fortnight."

"Only five hundred!"

"But think what that means; if I go on at this rate, in a couple of months I shall have nothing."

"Toto," said Gaillard earnestly, "I speak to you as a friend: Why pursue this course? Were I an enemy of yours I would urge you on, and then, when you came to grief, laugh at your sufferings.

I am your friend, and I say stop.   You are a fine
artist, and for that very reason you must fail in this
course.   Genius was never intended to buffet with
the world, to pay rent and fight with tradespeople;
it is always allied to a fine nature, and I predict the
most horrible sufferings for you should you continue this fictitious and insane battle with the
world.   It is only the duffers and the dullards who
succeed in this game; they have blunt noses, and
they do not feel blows.   Look at De Nani, a miserable wreck without an idea, of whom all Paris is
talking.   Look at me.   Could I tell you one-half
the hardships I have undergone in my struggle for
art, you would stop your ears.   Well, then, I say
desist; you can only live once: why make a hell of
life?   Come back to us; you have made an experiment in life.   It is like a curious philosophical experiment that dirties one's hands; well, then, let us
wash our hands, and turn down our cuffs again."

"Even if I wanted to stop this life, which I do
not," said Toto, playing with Gaillard's bait, " I
couldn't—sooner do anything than that."

"Nobody knows; it's a matter between you and

your conscience; *I* will never speak. You come back from Corsica in a hurry; well, what of that? it is a whim, and admirably in keeping with your character. Do, for Heaven's sake, Toto, consider your position; and mine, for I feel that I am in some sort responsible for this act of yours, but I have been at least discreet, and, as I said before, nobody knows."

" My mother knows."

" What is a mother, if not a confidante of our little eccentricities? "

" And the American girl knows."

" What! that American girl—would you give her a second thought? *Mon Dieu!* this is very funny. Oh, *mon Dieu!* this will kill me. An American pork butcheress; you told me yourself she was a pork butcheress. You are afraid of the jeers of this tripe-seller's daughter. I passed to-day three American women in green veils; they were promenading the Rue St. Honoré, and screaming through their noses; they had alpenstocks, or at least little sticks, adorned with horn handles and branded ' Rigi Kulm,' ' Rigi Scheideck.' They had ascended the Rigi, and were announcing the fact to the Rue St. Honoré; that is your American woman. They had faces like dollars, and for people like these you would inconvenience yourself."

" I tell you I don't want to go back. I am perfectly happy, perfectly contented. Don't talk any more about it. And I wish you would not call me Toto."

Gaillard turned the conversation to his own immediate wants, and the process of extraction was resumed till he had salved five hundred francs from this derelict, promising upon his honor to pay it back in three weeks. And scarcely had the money changed hands than Célestin entered, her arms full of parcels, and accompanied by Garnier. He had met her shopping, and accompanied her home, it being Saturday.

Then the poet took his departure, chuckling to himself about Garnier and the obvious worship of the big Provençal for the pretty Célestin; but for all that, he felt desperately uneasy about Toto. This foolishness might linger on for months like typhoid, and the best part of the year was coming on. At Christmas Toto had talked of hiring a steam yacht for the summer, and now this wretched Célestin and this vile art craze had spoiled it all. He could have wept as he walked hurriedly down the Rue de Perpignan looking for a cab to bear him to civilization, and after an absinthe, which acted on his trouble as stimulants on an abscess, heightening the inflammation and bringing it to a head, he sought Struve out in his rooms.

Struve was working in his shirt-sleeves at that book of his which made such a sensation a year later, " The Saint in Art."

" I am very uneasy about Toto."

" What's wrong with him? Has he been butted by a moufflon? "

" Toto is not in Corsica; Toto is in Paris."

" Oh, he's come back, is he? "

" Do attend to me, Struve. Toto is in an attic."

" What is he doing in an attic? "

" He is painting pictures."

" Has he gone mad? "

" No, he is not mad; but I fear he will make a very great fool of himself."

"I always said he would do that," granted Struve, examining attentively a tiny colored picture of St. Cecilia that was destined to adorn " The Saint in Art."

" I fear, if he is not stopped, he will make a very great mess of himself. He has taken only three thousand francs of his patrimony, and he swears that if he does not succeed on it he will cut his throat."

" You don't mean to say he has gone on with that foolishness? " asked Struve, leaning back in his chair and putting his hands in his pockets.

" I do indeed. It is a great piece of madness; but what is to be done? "

" Leave him alone."

" But he will starve to death."

" A little starvation will do him a lot of good; he has too much kick in him. The man is tired of playing the devil. He has tried everything, and now he is trying work. He will be back in a fortnight, a greater devil than ever. I like Toto. He is such a fool; but it's rather a pity. You see, he is a moon, and he wants to be a sun. He is tired of shining by the reflected glory of his fortune, and he wants to shine by his own light. He hasn't any to shine by, and there you are."

"He has certainly no genius, but he is a very facile painter."

"Facile rubbish! He can't paint."

"Do you not think, Otto, if you were to call upon him, and speak to him, and explain——"

"*Gott im Himmel!* what do you think my time is made for? Here am I behindhand with my book, and Flammarion like a caged tiger waiting for it. Go and tell his mother, go and tell his aunt, go to the devil, go anywhere, but don't bother me about it. I have no time to be running after Totos; I am not a wet-nurse. Go and get a perambulator and wheel him home. How is *Pantin?*"

"*Pantin* is very well. Has not Pelisson offered you the art criticisms?"

"Yes; but I am too busy to be bothered by *Pantins.*"

"You are right. Pelisson makes a rotten editor; he gives out books for review as if they were clothes for wash. And De Nani——"

"I know; he is an old fool. But do leave me now, like a good fellow," lisped Struve. "My head is so full of saints, it has no room for De Nanis."

Gaillard went off in a huff, but at the entresol returned to borrow a few cigarettes, for Struve's cigarettes were a dream.

"I forgot to tell you," said Gaillard as he lighted one, "not to say a word to anyone about Toto and his attic; he made me swear to tell no one."

"Then why did you tell me, you infernal idiot!" cried Struve, half laughing, yet nearly weeping at all these interruptions to his work.

"I quite forgot," said Gaillard, running off to confide his troubles to someone else, whilst the critic locked his door and bolted it.

The poet turned into the offices of *Pantin* in the Rue Drouot.

Since the birth of the new journal Pelisson had been pestered with a rain of old friends whom he had not seen for years, and some of whom he had never seen before. They all wanted employment,

or, failing that, a loan. Gaillard's long-suffering
creditors, hearing that he was on the staff, all appeared seeking for their money—a procession as
infinite as the Leonids, and on a business as apparently futile. The unfortunate Pelisson had also to
supervise his leader writers, write leaders himself,
and, worst of all, select the subjects. For this purpose he had to keep one eye fixed steadily upon the
whole world—that is to say, Paris. The other eye
was fully occupied by De Nani, who had caught on
most amazingly. Everyone was craving to see De
Nani. They saw glimpses only of him, and that
made them crave to see more. De Nani's white
hat loomed mysteriously above *Pantin;* his caustic
and cutting witticisms circulated in salon and club.
Quite a number of old gentlemen took to wearing
white hats and making cutting remarks about their
wives, and in the Rue St. Honoré one might see
De Nani waistcoats by the score. Kuhn's window
in the Rue de Rivoli exposed his portrait, the white
hat tilted to one side above the fiendish old face.
It was bought by the hundred, and Gaillard, like
a periodic comet, turned up at this window daily

to grit his teeth with anguish and envy and walk on with rage in his heart.

Pelisson was right. He had caught an old wether and belled it, and the crowd followed like the proverbial sheep. But the bell-wether required incessant watching; besides, De Nani during the last forty years had improved borrowing into one of the fine arts, and he was taking a thousand francs a day out of *Pantin* in various legitimate and illegitimate ways. He tapped Pelisson, he tapped the staff, he had established a credit at three cafés, he tapped the proprietors. He came east every morning from Auteuil as an American farmer comes to his maple trees, or a physician to a hospital for dropsy. He patronized three tailors, and bundles of clothes were constantly being left at the offices of *Pantin;* in fact, he seemed to be laying in a store of clothes, not only for this life, but for the next.

"I wonder he does not get a coffin as well to complete the outfit," said Gaillard once, viciously.

No doubt he would if he could have got a silver one to melt. He made up for his abstinence, however, in this respect by jewelry, scent, cosmetics, cigars, knickknacks, China mandarins, and varnished boots. It was not altogether his fault, for the tradesmen rushed upon him.

Pelisson did not much care what he got on credit, for he was editor only in name. If he lasted over the season it would be quite enough, for *Pantin* would then be well rooted, and any fiasco of bankruptcy would only make *Pantin* bloom the more. One might fancy that the bankruptcy of the editor would shake the paper in the eyes of the bourgeoisie, but the wise Pelisson knew better. "There is nothing," said he, "that a tradesman enjoys more than seeing another tradesman let in."

Pantin, be it observed, was now read, not only by the shopkeepers, but by the *beau monde*. Through its starch people observed a secret spirit at work. Its heavy sledge-hammer articles were supposed to be molding a crown. The journal was evidently a hit at the existing state of things; it was also strangely well informed, and the Ministry felt somewhat as a master might feel who suspected his butler of being a rogue, but could not prove the fact.

Amidst De Nani's other vagaries, affairs with

women figured chief, so you may imagine Pierre Pelisson had his hands full, and no ears for Gaillard's tale of tribulation about Toto. But De Nani had; he was sitting in a room adjoining the inner office, and heard the whole story—everything, in fact, but Toto's address.

CHAPTER III.

THE SORROWS OF ART.

LIKE Pelisson, the atelier in the Rue de Perpignan had its limitations; like Pelisson, it was also at times noisy. From the Gare de Sceaux at night and in the early morning came the sounds of shunting and the plaintive " toot-toot " of locomotives, whilst the top light seemed the chosen rendezvous of all the cats of the neighborhood who were in love.

" Those frightful cats! " would murmur Célestin, trembling beside Toto lest his sleep should be broken.

There were also draughts not specified in the lease, and the sink had a habit of getting stopped up at least once a day; then there was sometimes a smell of cooking from the rooms below.

Toto grumbled a little sometimes, but not much at first. The new life was so entirely different from the life he had led heretofore, so free, and withal so joyous, that for a little while he did not trouble himself as to the morrow. The only rose leaf that disturbed his rest during the first fortnight was the atelier of Melmenotte—art, in short.

Melmenotte had the air and aspect of a *vieux sabreur*. He inspected a picture as an infantry colonel inspects a regiment of the line, generally with a frown, sometimes with a few cutting words, sometimes with dead silence. He had inspected Toto's attempts with a damnatory sniff and passed on.

For this reason Toto avoided the atelier on the days when Melmenotte went round; for this reason, though he had dwelt now with art only a fortnight, he had, when Gaillard made his proposition of return, almost nibbled àt it. Melmenotte and his crew had somewhat disillusioned him. They were such a coarse lot. Their conversation was generally silly, sometimes absolutely vile; they pelted him with bits of bread when Garnier was not looking, and even the little loans he made to them did not buy him much esteem. It leaked out that his father had a shop; not that that fact would have in-

fluenced the students much one way or the other
had he possessed talent, but, lacking talent, they
saw in him an inevitable counter-jumper, and as a
result would have made his life a misery to him but
for Garnier, whose word was law, both on questions of art and conduct.

But Célestin knew nothing of these worries.
She knew nothing and cared nothing about anything except Toto; she did not even know his surname, for, though he had told it to her once, she
had forgotten it.

Neither did she inquire about his past. She
knew in a vague sort of way that he had always
lived in Paris, studying art, and being without
guile, as a flower, she never made that hackneyed
old inquiry, "Tell me, have you ever loved a woman before?"—to be answered by that hackneyed
old lie, "Never." Then, with that instinct which
orders what we might call the good manners of
love, she never loved him to weariness; she knew
the psychological moment for a kiss, the right time
for silence, and when to get upon his knee and
cheer him up, and talk to him in the language she

used to Dodor.   Always pretty, she had almost in a night become beautiful.   Toto had presented her with this added charm, but he did not perceive it; this extra beauty made up for the amount she had lost by surrendering herself to him.

One day Mme. Liard called to see how they were getting on, and brought a box of Choiseul's cough lozenges for Célestin as a sort of wedding gift. The good woman was greatly taken with the atelier, the couch which she sat on to sample and declared to be a marvel, and the great empty canvas on one of the easels.

"That is for his great picture," said Célestin proudly.   "Isn't it beautiful? and will it not be large?   And see our tulip"—pointing to the flower in the pot, which had burst into bloom.   "Is it not beautiful?   But Dodor is so jealous of it."

"Tulips die so soon," said Mme. Liard, who was a bit of a pessimist.   "Give me a double geranium. But flowers—bless you! I cannot keep them, for no sooner do I get a flower than Mimi scratches it up."

"Ah, Mimi!" said Célestin; "tell me how she is."

And Mme. Liard plunged into the inexhaustible subject of her cat.

Gaillard came down on them now and then like the wolf on the fold, and ate up a gread deal of provisions. In return, he taught them how to make coffee and told them fairy tales. He also borrowed little sums at parting, but that goes without saying. He also acted as a sort of intermediary between Toto and his mamma, and one day he brought them a ham from that lady, omitting to mention from whence it had come, presenting it as a gift of his own, in fact, and borrowing an extra five francs on the strength of it. He also brought to the Rue de Perpignan all his troubles, including the books for review doled out by Pelisson, and horrible stories about De Nani. The " Fall of the Damned " had been furiously attacked by a friend in the columns of the *Libre Parole*, yet it was far from flourishing. He brought a copy dressed in a fawn-colored wrapper, and adorned with red devils tumbling head over heels, and presumably into the pit.

" The cover," said Gaillard, " has spoiled the

sale a good deal. You have no idea of the influence of a cover on a book: devils have gone out of
fashion in the last month. It's all owing to that
exposure of the Satanists—silly fools!—and of
course it is just my luck, for I have a little brochure
in proof called ' Bon Jour, Satan.' Well, then, I
must change the title, and what does that mean?
Why, rewriting the book. People are turning religious, it seems; that is where art hits one. The
silly public takes a whim into its head; the artist
must meet it or starve. I had a meeting with
Chauvin, my publisher, to-day. You should have
seen his face. He declares the market for poetry
is dead, and the silly fool wants me to write him
something manly and religious. We nearly came
to words, but we made it up. I am actually like a
rat in a horrible trap. Do, Toto, act as a friend in
this matter, and till the end of the month, when my
royalties are due——"

"It is absolutely disgusting," Gaillard would
murmur to himself as he made for home after these
expeditions. "It is like asking a loan from a
laborer. He takes out a few francs and looks at

them as if they were his last, and that little Célestin,
I believe she puts him up to resist lending; I believe she puts all his spare money into the money-
box of that wretched lark.   I believe she is in love
with that great fat beast who smells of garlic, and
who always runs away when I come, as if he feared
the presence of a gentleman; that is the lark she is
saving up for.   Yes, some day Toto will wake up
to find nothing but a smell of garlic and Célestin
flown.   It will serve him right."

Yet, were Toto out when he called at the atelier,
he would lay his troubles on the back of Célestin,
always sure of attention and commiseration.   And
smoking his eternal cigarettes, he would pour into
her ear the horrors of life, the futility of Pelisson,
the detestable nature of De Brie, and the villainy
of De Nani.   Sometimes Toto, returning after one
of these séances had lasted an hour or so, would
find Célestin looking almost old, and with tears in
her heavenly eyes.

" I have been telling her a society fairy tale,"
would say Gaillard.

CHAPTER IV.

BOURGEOIS—BANKER—PRINCE.

IT was now June, and lately Toto had become subject to moods, or, to speak more correctly, fits of moodiness. He had now for a month or more been living face to face with Art, and the prolonged interview with that lady was bearing fruit in his manners and customs.

Three weeks ago he would not have cared very much had Paris known of his mode of life and ridiculed him for it. Cocksure, and blinded by the *fata Morgana* of success, he would have shaken his palette in the face of Paris; but Art had changed all that.

" Art is not a wanton, to be hired for a night," said Garnier one day in answer to a remark of Toto's. " *Mon Dieu!* no; she is like that woman in the Bible whose courting took seven years, and then again seven years, and seven years again. Work, and don't think, work and don't think."

Easy advice to give. Toto was now continually thinking. He was in a worse Bastille than that from which Latude made his escape, for he had devised his own bondhouse, and the prison a man makes for himself is of all prisons, perhaps, the most difficult to leave.

He dreaded now meeting anyone that he knew, and in the street going to and from the studio glanced about him with the eyes of a frightened hare. As yet no one knew of his folly but Gaillard, Helen Powers, and his mother, but, indeed, that audience, together with his self-respect, were quite enough to keep him performing a little while longer.

Then there was Célestin. The unutterable contentment and bliss of Célestin with her new life filled the heart of Toto sometimes now with a vague sort of terror. She seemed to think that this sort of thing was to go on forever. Her love for him, expressed in a thousand different ways, seemed to spring from infinity itself, and love like this is to the beloved either a blessing beyond all blessings or a curse. To Toto just now it was not a blessing.

Of course, by a cab to the Nord, or the L'Ouest, or the Orleans railway, and a ticket to anywhere, and a few months' absence, he could have put everything to rights. Paris, like a cold gray sea, would have washed over Célestin and Dodor, washed away the furniture of the atelier, washed away his memory from the *rapins* at Melmenotte's, and obliterated all traces. Paris, whose motto is "I have forgotten," would not trouble even to repeat those funereal and final words over this small escapade.

But Toto was not the person to leave Célestin and Dodor to the mercies of Paris. In some unaccountable way Célestin had drawn the better parts of his nature to herself; to wound her would be to wound himself. If he thought Célestin were weeping alone in some attic, it would have taken the pleasure from life, and spoiled his digestion, and filled his nights with nightmares, for his better parts would have been weeping with her. In short, though capable of a foolish action, he was as yet incapable of a ruffianly, and as a result he was unhappy. A perfectly happy fool must always, I think, be a ruffian.

One day Garnier, who called frequently now as a friend of the family, found Célestin on the verge of tears. The tulip in the red-tile pot had died, and she was inconsolable. She declared that she would never keep another when Garnier offered to replace it.

"Never mind," said the painter; "I will procure you a flower that will not die."

A juggler who had lodged once in the same house had instructed him in the manufacture of roses that never die, immortal tulips, and decay-defying camellias. They were made from turnips cunningly carved and dyed in cochineal. Camellias were the easiest to make, roses more difficult, whilst tulips, strange to say, were the most difficult of all. The tulip had first to be blocked out roughly from the succulent root; then the exterior had to be carved, and lastly, the whole thing hollowed neatly.

So Garnier took a day off, and procured a turnip and a knife, some cochineal, and all the other necessary paraphernalia, and, with his work cut out before him, locked his door. This room of Garnier's was close to the roof, and from its window one could see the spires of Notre Dame by standing on a chair. A desperate-looking cat lived here, whose life had been saved by the artist one morning as he was starting to work. It had repaid him lately by kittening under his bed. In one corner of the room lay a pile of newspapers, on the chimney-piece some books—Rousseau's " Nouvelle Héloïse " in paper covers; a little book of German fairy tales, which he could not read, but which he treasured because of the delightful pictures; " The Mysteries of Paris," which he had read four times; and a few others.

On this floor also there was a large atelier kept up by three young men from the South, who did their own cooking, so that the place was always filled with the sound of frying and the smell of garlic. They did their own washing, too, and so defied the laundress; they also at times defied the landlord when he threatened to turn them out. They had got an old banjo from somewhere, and, needless to say, they played on it. Garnier worked in this atelier when he was not working elsewhere. He loved its discords, and never painted better than when Castanet was playing the banjo, Lorillard accompanying him on a comb, and Floquet frying things over the stove, for then he imagined himself back in Provence, and the atelier became flooded with the light that never was in Paris except on the canvas of a Diaz or a Garnier.

Floquet had a sweetheart, who sat to him for love, and of course also to his friends. She darned Castanet's stockings, for he wore them out in some miraculous way quicker than anyone else. As for Lorillard, he never wore stockings—at least, in summer—and laughed at people who did.

Altogether they were as disreputable a colony as one could find in the whole quarter, but as good-hearted as they were jolly. Castanet, be it observed, was a law student; he lived with the others just as the owl lives with the prairie-dogs, because he liked them.

All these people noticed a change that had come over Garnier during the last fortnight. He was abstracted, he sighed, he laughed at nothing, burst out laughing sometimes as he painted, in a happy manner, as if a child had performed some antic for his amusement, and then a few minutes later he would give a little groan. He no longer cast his brushes joyously aside when Floquet turned the shrieking and fizzing pan of fish stewed in garlic onto a dish; his appetite had diminished.

The fact was, the great Garnier was miraculously in love. When an elephant falls into a pit he does it in a whole-hearted manner; so fell Garnier into this passion. Célestin had been for him that dangerous thing—a revelation. She had eclipsed the *Intransigèant*, and robbed Henri Rochefort of his power; she had touched Prince Rudolph, and he had slunk back into his impossible mysteries; she had taken the charm from garlic, and even the wizard café lost its fascination.

Yet for all this he was not in love with Célestin in the ordinary acceptation of the term. He never dreamt of marriage with her, simply because during the last twelve days he had become miraculously married to her. She dwelt with him always now in that atelier he called his head. There she made her hats, trimming them with sunbeams, and turning to him for admiration with her celestial smile.

She was the wife of his soul. Never was there a purer passion begotten of man and woman; yet, strangely enough, it did not purify him. He talked of women in the same old free-and-easy way, and the jokes of Castanet, Lorillard, Floquet & Co. did not shock him.

Had Célestin lived in a romance, she would doubtless have cast her light on womanhood. She would have elevated Garnier, and he certainly would have been none the worse for that. In reality, however, her effulgence showed him nothing but herself.

She had such pretty ways. Her slightest movement had a deeply artistic meaning. She interpreted unspoken sentences with a motion of her hands. A poppy swaying in the wind had not the grace of Célestin crossing the floor to put the little kettle on the stove. Her talk seemed a strange sister of Dodor's song. And then the way she had of casting her eyes up to heaven! Her gaze always seemed to return bluer from that journey, and filled with light gathered from the ghostly distance.

She was all those twelve children he had longed for rolled into one, and much more besides. She was one of those delightful little cherubs over the fonts in the Church of St. Germain l'Auxerrois; she was the wind that waved the trees at Barbizon, the flowers that blew to the wind, and the sparrows that flew in the street; she was Mistigris, the cat who lived under his bed, and each of Mistigris's six kittens. For all of these things that he loved when he thought of, beheld, or felt them, reminded him of Célestin.

He labored away over his tulip, carving at it with infinite care. Castanet came and kicked at his door, and asked him what he was doing, and then he felt the eye of Castanet peering through the keyhole, and heard his voice informing Floquet that Garnier was writing a letter to his sweetheart. Then the banjo struck up, and the doleful sound of the comb laboring out " Partant pour la Syrie " mixed with the sound of Lorillard washing his shirt and beating it between his hands as a sort of accompaniment to the music.

Then the flower was at last accomplished—a bit too thick in the petal, perhaps, but still a fairly accurate representation. He dyed it with the cochineal, and mounted it on a little green stick he had prepared to do duty for a stalk. It was a poor child for so great an artist to produce, yet he smiled at it in a satisfied manner, for it reminded him of Célestin.

He then went to the atelier of Castanet & Co. to see if he could get a piece of fish for Mistigris, who had come out from under the bed with a kitten in her mouth, as if to remind him that she was the mother of a family and required sustaining. And when he had fed her, he darted off with the tulip in his hand, making for the Rue de Perpignan, regardless of the ribaldry of his compatriots, who were watching him from their window away up near the roof. He hurried along like a man pursuing fortune, or as if fearful that the tulip would wither.

Toto was out, but Célestin was at home mending a glove.

" Ah, *ciel!* " cried Célestin, as she held the tulip out between finger and thumb. " What a marvelous thing! You made it, and from a turnip! It is a miracle!"

" We will plant it!" cried Garnier, running about with the red-tile pot in his hand, and looking for some place in which to throw the dead flower. There was a sink outside the door; he cast it there.

Then they planted the new tulip, pressing the mold tightly around the base of the stick, and hardly was the thing accomplished when Toto entered, looking worried, and as if he had been walking in a hurry.

" Yes, it is very nice," said Toto in the manner of an absent-minded parent as they called upon him to admire their handiwork.

He kissed Célestin without fervor, and then, pulling Garnier aside by the arm, invited him to come outside for a moment and have a glass of beer, and give his advice about a picture.

" I have had a row at the studio," said Toto, when they were in the street.

" Eh! what? with Melmenotte? "

" No, that fool Jolly. I knocked him down."

" What! you did that? *Boufre!* but it will do him a lot of good, that same Jolly. I have often wished to do so myself, but I am too big, and he is too small. You are more of his size. And why did you knock him down? "

" He told me I wasn't able to paint, that any *demi-mondaine* had more art in painting her face than I had in painting a picture."

" But that is nothing; we all tell each other things like that."

" Yes, but he meant it; and, he said it in such an insulting manner, and, besides, he only said it because I had refused to lend him more money."

" So you knocked him down! " cried Garnier, breaking into a roar of laughter. " *Mon Dieu!* and I missed it! I would have given five francs to have been there."

They entered a little café, and Toto called for two bocks.

" I am very unhappy," said Toto as he sipped his beer.

" What! about that rascal Jolly? "

" Oh, no; it is not that.   I am unhappy about a lot of things.   I wish I had never come to the Rue de Perpignan."

" Oh! "

" Yes, tell me something seriously.   How long do you think it will be before I am able to exhibit? "

Garnier shifted about in his seat.   He did not know exactly what to say; he had never considered Toto's art seriously.   His father had a shop, and the son, after dabbling a while with art, would doubtless end happily behind the counter.   He was having his *Wanderjahr* now.   Even at the worst he might become a great artist.   Who could tell?   And who was Garnier that he should throw water on another man's aspirations?

" Five years," said Garnier.   " You see, you are only beginning.   The great thing in art is time; nothing is done without time and patience.   Another thing: one must not think.   Work away and don't think. Don't ask 'How am I getting on?' or, at least, only on New Year's Day. Then, enjoy yourself, and keep your eyes open. Paris is a big atelier. An artist wants to study movement as well as the nude. I never walk down the street but I pick up something; it all comes in handy. If you want to paint life, you must dip your brush in everything, even mud. Those old men who spent their lives painting pots and pans and saints leave me cold. I would like to clap the Rue St. Honoré into a canvas—will, too, some day. I don't think there is anything more fine in nature than a fire-engine going full speed to a fire, except, maybe, a dragon-fly."

Garnier buried his nose in his glass, and Toto put his chin on his palm, his elbow on the table, and stared before him, as if gazing at a cheerless view.

" Or a girl flinging up her arms to yawn," continued Garnier. "Girls are all art—that is why they make such rotten artists; but they are natural when they are flinging up their arms to yawn, or stooping to tie their garters, because then they think no one is looking at them, or they don't care."

He held out a handful of cigarettes, and Toto took one.

"I have never seen Célestin yawn," said Toto in a meditative voice, as he lit the cigarette.

"Heavens! no," said Garnier.

"Why not?"

"The gift of weariness is not given to her. Have you ever seen a butterfly yawn, or a happy child?"

"She *is* happy!" said Toto in a half-regretful voice.

"She is happiness, you mean. *Mon Dieu!* yes, she is happiness; as for me, when I see her I always feel ten years younger, twenty years younger when she speaks, thirty years younger when she smiles."

"You are only twenty-five."

"Oh, yes; so you see, Mlle. Célestin's smile puts me back to five years before my birth. I was then an angel, a fat little angel in the cherub cage; there I would have been still had not the Father Eternal put in his hand and taken me out, and flung me to the blue, crying 'Try your wings.' That is how the business is managed: the world is pursued by a flock of cherubs in search of a roost; when they overtake the world, they take it by storm, people want to marry, and that makes spring; when the world outstrips them that makes winter. I have never begotten a child, so I have never given a perch to one of those sparrow angels, worse luck!" and Garnier sighed and called for more beer.

"Shall I tell you something?" asked Toto, who had been slowly making up his mind as the painter prattled.

"Why, yes!"

"Well, you remember, when I met you first, you asked me what my father was. I said he had a shop. Well, I told you a lie."

"*Ma foi!* why not? What do I care what your father is?—you are a good fellow. That is enough for me. We all boast a bit, we artists."

"I was not exactly boasting," said Toto, knocking the ash off his cigarette in a nervous manner. "My father made all his money out of a bank."

"You don't mean to say he is a banker!" said

"*Mon Dieu!* what a funny man you are! What is there pleasanter to meet than a friend?"

"Yes; but don't you understand? I don't want my friends to know that I am an artist."

"And, for Heaven's sake, why not?"

"Well, for one thing, they would laugh at me."

"Laugh at you for being an artist! Sacred Heaven! what a funny man you are, and what funny friends you must have! And why should they laugh at you for being an artist?"

"Well, you see, they don't know anything about art, for one thing."

"Ah, I can see those friends of yours!" said Garnier, with an inspired air. "Old religious ladies, aunts, and what not,—they drive in carriages with pug dogs,—and old gentlemen with the Legion of Honor."

"Not at all; my friends are quite young."

"Who are they, then?"

"Well, there is Eugène Valfray, son of the railway man."

"Never heard of him."

"Then there is the Prince de Harnac—Gustave."

"What, you know a Prince!"

"Why, man, I am a Prince."

"You are a what?"

"I am a Prince," said Toto shamefacedly.

"Ah, *mon Dieu!* what a droll you are!" cried Garnier, breaking into a laugh. "First you are a bourgeois, then you are a banker, then you are a Prince."

"I am not joking; I am what I say."

"But," cried Garnier, sobered by the serious face of Toto, "you a Prince, sitting here at the Trois Frères with me! Come now! a joke is all very well up to a certain point; beyond that it makes one feel giddy. Besides, you are not like a Prince."

"For Heaven's sake, what *is* a Prince like?" asked Toto, half laughing, half vexed. "I have never seen a Prince that was different from anyone else; they are generally more stupid, perhaps, but that is all."

"But what are you Prince of?" cried the

painter, belief and disbelief battling in his mind.

"My father was a prince of the Roman Empire. I am the same, of course, now that he is dead."

"But, my dear child!" cried the Provençal, to whom a Prince was a Prince, no matter what empire he belonged to, "what made you come amongst us at Melmenotte's? it is like what one reads in a romance, all this. I could not have believed it. And what made you come to live in the Rue de Perpignan? And Célestin! Ah, *ciel!* I see it all now: she is a Princess; that is what makes her different from other people. A Princess! she has made me coffee, whilst I have talked to her as to a child. I have carved for her a tulip out of a turnip, and I never guessed who she was, when it was plain before me written all over her——"

"You are wrong," said Toto in a troubled voice. "She is not a Princess; I wish she were. Listen, my friend, and I will tell you all. I want your advice."

He told the little story of his meeting with Célestin, everything; he sketched rapidly a portrait of his mother; then he paused to let the tale sink in, and Garnier rubbed his chin.

" But what made you do all this? " asked the painter at last. " You could have painted at home."

" I don't know; I was so sick of it all. I wanted a change, I wanted to do for myself; it seemed so jolly to have an atelier, and live in a blouse and work; then, besides—I can't explain exactly, but I felt as if I wanted to grow: a lot of people had de- ceived me. They did not mean it, I suppose, but they praised my work; besides, I felt that they were laughing at me behind my back."

He told the story of De Nani, and the truth that had escaped from him in drink; he felt no shame in confiding his troubles to Garnier. All great- minded people have this in common. They resem- ble priests; we confess to them openly what we would not whisper to little minds.

" Ah, well," said Garnier, " there are rogues in every trade, and that old man is a rogue. *Mon Dieu!* I am not straitlaced; but there are

two things I cannot stand by and see: an
old man drunk, and an old man following
a woman. Do not think of him, but tell
me now, what does it feel like to be a Prince?
Oh, I should like to be a Prince just for an hour!
I would dress myself in ermine and walk down the
Rue de Rivoli. Ah! you are laughing, but I would.
I would call my servants and give them orders,
just to hear them call me M. le Prince. I would
call at Melmenotte's, and walk about the atelier
trailing my skirts. *Mon Dieu!* yes, I should like to
be a Prince just for an hour."

"And then?"

"Oh, I would kick off my togs and come back
and be an artist. Just as you will kick off your
togs and go back to be a Prince; one always re-
turns to one's trade."

"You think I will go back to be a Prince?"

"Why, of course."

"Would you advise me to?"

"Why, of course, when you are tired of your
atelier you will put on your crown."

"I have no crown," said Toto; "but I will no

doubt return and put on a tall hat. What troubles me is Célestin."

" Ah! Célestin!"

" She does not know who I am."

Garnier frowned slightly.

" She would not have loved me, I think, if I had told her, poor child! She has a great awe of titled people; she makes hats for them. She will never do that again, anyhow."

" Still," said Garnier, " you ought to have told her."

" Why? I don't see why."

" You have told me, yet you would hide what I know from that angel of light. That is not as it should be. Take it as a man. How would you like Mlle. Célestin to deceive you? The thing is impossible, but, still——"

" Perhaps you are right; and I wish I had never met her."

Garnier frowned again.

" You do not love her, then?"

" Oh, yes; I do. It is not that, but my mother, and all the people I know. Not that I care a button—not a button; let them all go to the devil."

"Ah, now you speak like a man! And will you tell Célestin all that you have told to me?"

"I will. I will tell her this evening."

But when evening came, and he sat alone with Célestin on the couch in the lamplight, and when he took her hand saying "I want to tell you something; I ought to have told it to you before," the words dried up; he could not tell her of his position in the world; besides, he knew her inevitable answer, "What matter, so long as we love each other?" It always came when difficulties arose— if the beef was understewed or the wine sour, if the cats kept them awake or if the door of Dodor's cage got jammed.

"Célestin, I ought to have told you before; but do you know that, though we live here in this atelier and are happy enough, God knows—do you know that I am—awfully poor?"

"What matter? what does anything matter, so long as we love each other?" sighed Célestin.

"I will tell you all about myself some day," said Toto. "I have not told you I have a mother."

"Ah, how I would love to see her! How happy, that is, to have a mother! As for me, I never had a mother."

"Perhaps it is just as well you had not."

"I will tell you," said Célestin: "we will share your mother. I will take one-half of her heart, and you will have the other, like those ogres in that fairy tale of dear M. Gaillard's."

"Thanks," said Toto; "you may have it all."

" DODOR, we are very poor," said Célestin next morning. She had taken the lark from its cage, and was holding the little warm, brown body to her breast.

Toto had gone out to slink about the streets in a miserable state of mind. He was deadly tired of his atelier—Art had pulled his ears; yet he was ashamed to go home. Besides, how about Célestin?

He felt like a child who had stolen a fiddle, unable to play on it, tired of it, afraid to return it, and wavering for a moment ere he throws it into the nearest ditch. It was ten o'clock in the morning.

" So," continued Célestin, putting the lark back in its cage, " I am going to make some money."

Her head was full of echoes begotten of Toto's words last night, " I am very poor," and plans begotten of the echoes. She had all her life been well-to-do; by some special provision of God's, instead of her seeking work, work had always stolen to seek her fingers; the winds had blown tulle and artificial roses across her path; Mme. Hümmel had supplied her with foundations, and art had done the rest.

So it was a new sensation to hear the wolf scratch at the door, rather fearful, yet almost pleasurable: for was not Toto with her, and so long as they loved each other what did anything matter?

She had three hats finished—four, in fact, but only three for sale. For the fourth was the one she had made that morning,—the morning of the honeymoon,—and it was not for sale. She could not think of allowing another woman to wear it, so she put it on her head, determining to wear it herself.

She had on a dress of lilac-colored nun's cloth. She made the three hats up in a parcel, and then drew on a pair of lilac-colored gloves.

"How grand Mme. Hümmel will think I have become!" said Célestin, as she departed.

Even the old Rue de Perpignan looked young
this morning. It was a blissful and dreamy day;
heavy showers had fallen in the early morning,
leaving a perfume in the air, faint, as if from the
gardens of Paradise.

She reached Verral's in the Rue St. Honoré
without any surprising adventure, and entered by
the side door that leads to the workrooms. These
lay behind the showrooms, the buzz and murmur
of which penetrated the thin partitions dividing the
one from the other. The atmosphere was warm
and filled with that oppressive smell which comes
from millinery in a mass. Size, varnish, and glue
contributed their odors, whilst the air vibrated with
the whir of sewing machines from the rooms
above.

" Ah, the little Célestin! " cried Mme. Hümmel,
a stout Alsatian in black silk, and with a good-natured face.

" I sent a girl to the Rue de Babylone only last
week to see if you were dead, and they said you
were married. Bad child not to have told me! I
was frightened. I could not sleep at night, say-

ing to myself, 'Where is that Célestin?' So you have brought me some hats?"

She led the way to her private room, and looked at the hats, and praised them a little: for it does not do to lavish praise on employees; they are apt to wax fat on it and kick for higher prices, as Mme. Hümmel had learnt in the course of her experience.

Then she ran away to get some money, and Célestin stood by the table, on which lay feathers, patterns of silk, and those *pompons* which, according to Gaillard, were the mainstay and support of the mysterious Angélique.

" This is for the work," said Mme. Hümmel, paying the stipulated amount, " and this is for yourself. It is a wedding gift. Poor child! are you happy?"

" Oh, very happy!" said Célestin, putting the napoleon just given to her for a wedding gift into her glove, and the six francs into her purse. " Happier than I can tell. How good it is of you! A whole napoleon! I never thought—I——"

" No, do not thank me. You are a good child, and I am sure you will make him happy. You must bring him to see me some Saturday. I will lecture him for you. And is he dark or fair? and what is his name? "

" He is dark, and his name is Désiré."

" And his other name? "

" I don't know," said Célestin. " He told me once, and I have forgotten. How stupid it is of me! "

Mme. Hümmel smothered a little laugh.

" So you do not know his surname? *Mon Dieu!* what a droll child you are! "

" I don't remember it. My head will not hold names; it is like a sieve. I am very silly." And Célestin, blushing and shaking the good woman by the hand, departed, whilst Madame cried after her, " Be sure and bring him some Saturday for me to lecture him," little thinking that this young man with the forgettable surname was Toto, son of Verral's best customer, Mme. la Princesse de Cammora.

Célestin walked away, so lost in her napoleon that she did not notice the clouds hurrying up from the southwest. Like everything fortunate, the napoleon was a gift from the good God. Toto was one of these gifts, or, rather, the chief of them; and as she made her way along the busy street, she cast her eyes up several times as if returning thanks through the brim of her hat to those favored angels, her guardians.

A thought had crossed her mind. She would get a money-box for Toto and save up for him, for what would happen if she were to die, and he were left like the artist in that terrible play at the Porte St. Martin? Already, in fancy, she was supporting him by her hats whilst he pursued his beautiful art to fame.

But if she were to die? Her lips trembled. Those two children of hers, Toto and Dodor! They crossed her imagination together, feckless creatures, one so like the other in character, either jumping about on their perches, or moping, irresponsible, and terribly in need of someone to tidy their cages, talk to them, and love them.

She was passing a frightful criticism on Toto, but she did not know it. Perhaps the only people who criticise us justly are the people who love us, for our perfections and imperfections are to them all one country, and of that country perhaps our imperfections are the fairest part.

Just as she reached the middle of the Place de la Concorde the clouds burst. It was like a huge shower bath, of which the string had suddenly been pulled. In a second the Madeleine and Rue Royale on one hand, and the big letters announcing the Chamber of Deputies on the other, were veiled by sheets of rain.

Célestin awoke suddenly from her painful, half-pleasurable reverie, to find herself drenched. She had no umbrella, and her friends the omnibuses were not near, so she ran through sheets of rain, till her hat was ruined, and then she hid in a doorway, panting, and with her hand to her breast. The shower spent itself in ten minutes, and the day smiled out again brighter than ever. So she pursued her way to the Rue de Perpignan, wet to the skin, and rejecting the idea of an omnibus because of the expense for one thing, and, besides, she was wet already, and it was safer to walk and keep warm.

When she reached the atelier she found Toto carefully drying himself at the stove. He, too, had been caught by the rain, but not so badly.

She insisted upon his taking off his coat, and whilst it was drying she talked to him and laughed to cheer him up. Then she spread the cloth on the table, for it was time for *déjeuner*, and lastly she went to the bedroom, like a prudent person, and changed her things. But the beautiful hat was ruined beyond redemption, and as she gazed at it she gave a little shiver.

That evening, when the lamp was lit, she told Toto all about Mme. Hümmel, the selling of the hats, the gift of the napoleon, and the desire of the forewoman to see him and lecture him.

Toto listened half unconsciously. He was already revolving in his mind plans of escape from his cage. He had fixed upon Gaillard as the man of all others to help him, but he had not seen Gaillard now for four days.

As Célestin finished her story—she was sitting upon the floor, her head resting against Toto's knee—a shudder ran through her, and her teeth chattered.

"Why," cried Toto, "what is this? What makes you shiver so?"

"I don't know," said Célestin, half laughing. "I did not do it on purpose;" and again the rigor seized her, as if someone were shaking her by the shoulder. "I will go to bed," she said, rising to her feet. "My head swims."

"I hope she is not going to be ill," thought the Prince to himself. "And I do wish Gaillard would come. What can have happened to him?"

Part IV.

CHAPTER I.

ADAM FROISSART.

NOTHING in particular had happened to Gaillard, yet the poet was in tribulation. To begin with, all his friends were too busy to attend to or amuse themselves with him. Struve was writing his book, or, rather, correcting the proof sheets, an employment that kept him short of temper and time; Pelisson had only one idea—*Pantin;* Toto was crabbedly finding out his own stupidity in the Rue de Perpignan; whilst De Brie had turned very acid over his connection with the new journal, and flung him commissions for little articles or volumes for review as if they were bones to a dog.

Then his publisher had informed him, with a very long face, that only three hundred copies of " The Fall of the Damned " had sold in three weeks,

227

whereas three thousand of "Satanitie" had gone off in the same time.

To make matters worse, Papillard had stopped working; De Nani had frozen him. De Nani he felt to be the cause of all his misfortunes, and he only continued to exist—so he told himself—that he might witness De Nani's downfall.

You may imagine, then, how pleased he felt when, on the morning after the same showery day that drenched Célestin, Pelisson appeared in his rooms before eight o'clock, and pulled up his blinds.

"Wake up! I want Adam Froissart's address," cried Pelisson, standing over the poet, and poking him with his stick to rouse him.

"Froissart!" cried Gaillard, rubbing his eyes. "He is not in Paris."

"Where is he, then?"

"He is in—Amiens," said Gaillard.

Froissart was a spiteful genius who possessed the unsavory humor of Papillard. No one had ever seen him, and his sole title to consideration lay in three malevolent articles leveled against De Brie and his political tendencies. They had been sub-mitted to Pelisson by Gaillard, and so had found their way into the *Débats*. Pelisson, who noted down everything, had made a memorandum of this gentleman's abilities. De Brie had done likewise, and though he hated this unknown journalist, he would have given a good deal to secure him as a member of his staff. He had expressed the desire in the hearing of Gaillard, and he might have ob-tained his wish, only that Froissart's genius for malevolence was useless when expended against anyone else than De Brie.

Needless to say, there was no Froissart. He be-longed to the shadowy band that included Fanfoul-lard, Mirmillard, Papillard, Églantine, and Angé-lique.

" This is a great nuisance," grumbled Pelisson, rubbing his chin.

" What do you want of Froissart? "

" I am going to sack De Nani, and I want a man to take his place."

Gaillard's countenance became glorified.

" But, my dear Pierre, why seek for Froissart?

Are there not plenty of men of ability in Paris to take the place of this silly old villain of a De Nani? "

" Hundreds, but no use to me. I don't want one of your bright diamonds—I want a man in the rough; I don't want an editor—I want a creature, a clever one, too, now: for, upon my soul, I am becoming exhausted between keeping *Pantin* and De Nani going at the same time. You said this Froissart was poor."

" Frightfully."

" That's just what I want."

" But I believe he has an aunt who is very rich, and I heard she was dying some little time ago. I would not seek Froissart, Pierre; believe me, he is a very acid man, and quite unfit for an editor. If you want the sort of person you say you want, why not try me? I will do whatever you wish, and write whatever you wish."

" No, no! " cried Pelisson hastily; " it would not do. You are a poet—stick to your last. Besides, I have been bombarded with your creditors; I've had enough of that. That is one of the reasons I am sacking De Nani. The old fool has burst the bladder. Someone went to Auteuil to make inquiries, and found he was living in three rooms, and owed money to his laundress. You can fancy how the news has flown amongst his creditors. Next thing someone will find out that he is a fool."

" But why not edit the thing yourself? "

" So I do; but I want a shield. *Pantin* will begin to bellow soon. Well, no matter; I am off for Amiens. I won't be back till to-morrow. What's this man's address? "

" He lives in a cottage near the railway station; you will easily find it—there are roses on the porch. But, see here; who's taking charge till you return? "

" De Nani, nominally; he cannot do any harm in one day. Besides, I have left everything cut and dried."

" Does he know he is getting the sack? "

" I should think so. He and I have been at the office all night talking things over. He is quite resigned—going to cut and run. I left him asleep on the sofa. Now good-by. The cottage near the railway station, you say. *Mon Dieu!* I will scarcely have time to catch the train."

He darted off, and Gaillard sank down again in bed filled with the bliss of satisfied hatred. De Nani was down at last; the little world of æsthetic people who required " Satanities " and " Falls of the Damned " would now, perhaps, give their Gaillard undivided attention. He never once thought of Pelisson gone off on a wild-goose chase to Amiens, and soon he forgot even De Nani, immersed in visions of an impossible Gaillard worshiped by an impossible world.

Mme. Plon came in and placed *Pantin* on the foot of his bed, and a letter in a blue envelope. The letter looked like a bill, so he left it whilst he glanced at the journal with languid interest. Then he picked up the letter, which had been left by a messenger, and, to his surprise, found that it was from De Nani.

" My Dear M. Gaillard [said De Nani]: May I ask you to call upon me immediately on receipt of this? It is of the utmost importance that I should see you without a moment's delay."

It was written upon the office paper, bearing the stamp "*Pantin*, No. ——, Rue Drouot. Rédacteur, M. le Marquis de Nani. Cable and telegraphic address: 'Pouf.' Telephone: No. 1654320." Over all, the motto and watchword of the journal: "*Qui vive?*"

"Now, what can he want?" murmured Gaillard. "It is like his impertinence to send for me as if I were his footboy. I shall not go."

And he turned over on his side. But no mongoose was ever of a more inquisitive nature than our friend Gaillard. What could De Nani want, and without a moment's delay? He tried to imagine and failed, and then arose and dressed.

M. le Marquis de Nani was in the inner office. Since the night of Toto's dinner-party at the Grand Café he had grown fat, or, at least, decidedly fatter. His raiment was superb; he had adorned his stomach with a gold and platinum watch-chain. He wore a shawl waistcoat, and his cuff-links, of dull gold, were enameled with pictures of tiny champagne bottles and opera dancers.

He was standing before the indifferent looking-glass that adorned the mantel, examining his face and informing Scribe, the cashier, that *Pantin* had given him ten new wrinkles. A café near by had just sent in *déjeuner* for two and a bottle of Pommery.

"I am expecting M. Gaillard to breakfast," explained De Nani. "A most promising young man, whose interests I have at heart."

Scribe bowed and left the room. He was a shock-headed man, with musical instincts and a genius for figures; he held the Marquis in great reverence, and had an implicit faith in him that somewhat troubled Pelisson. Yet what could Pelisson do? You cannot tell the cashier to beware of the editor? This implicit faith of Scribe's was perhaps one factor in the sacking of De Nani, although goodness knows there were others enough.

"You sent for me, I believe," said Gaillard rather stiffly, as he entered the inner office and made a

little bow to his editor, whilst he glanced at the
nice little *déjeuner* on the table.

"*Ma foi*, yes; I trust you will excuse the
brusquerie of my note, my dear M. Gaillard. Will
you not join me at breakfast? That is right. I
will explain myself as we eat; we shall not be interrupted, for Pelisson has gone off somewhere for the
day."

"Pelisson will not be back till to-morrow," said
Gaillard, thawing visibly as he flung a bundle of
papers off a chair and took his seat at the table.
"He has gone to Amiens."

De Nani hid his satisfaction at this remark, as he
unwired the champagne. Then the two, hobnob-
bing across the table, shared a Perigord pie, and
conversation became general; it swiftly became in-
delicate, and then confidential.

"You are right," said the Marquis, in answer to
a remark dropped by his *vis-à-vis*. "Pelisson has
his limitations—ahu!"

"Pelisson is a journalist, a recorder of this ill-
written tragedy which we are condemned to act in,
and which we call, for want of a better name, 'life.'

Oh, this life that they are always prating about!
A scoundrel only the other day accused me of in-
sincerity to life.   Could he have paid me a higher
compliment? "

" No, egad.   Ha! the infernal scamp said that,
did he?   What will you have?—they must have
' copy '; that is the watchword of this villainous
world, that stinks of printer's ink.   ' Copy, copy '
—I will give them some copy.   A word in your
ear, M. Gaillard."

" I am all attention."

" I feel safe in admitting you into my little
secret, for you are a man of honor.   I feel safe in
admitting you into the secret of my little surprise,
inasmuch as it concerns Pelisson, who is not your
friend, M. Gaillard."

" Have you heard him saying things about me? "
asked Gaillard, who was under the fixed belief that
one half of the world spent its existence in slander-
ing his works to the other half."

" I have heard him say——"

" Yes? "

" No matter; what is the use of repeating the

words of a man like Pelisson—ahu! They are like the crackling of thorns under a pot, as that delightfully humorous book, the Bible, has it. I should not have mentioned the chattering of this magpie. Fill your glass, M. Gaillard."

" But, my dear Marquis, I implore you to tell me what this Pelisson has been uttering about me; it is always well to know one's friends."

" Well, egad, he said so much I have forgotten half of it. One day—it was last week—he said, ' This Gaillard thinks himself a poet.' Harmless words, but it was the tone of his voice that set all the office laughing. I did not laugh, it was bad form; but there is no form in this journalistic world. I am leaving it, I have had words with Pelisson; and before I take my departure it is my humble ambition to make Pierre Pelisson dance."

" He ought to be dancing on an organ," said Gaillard in a bitter voice. " It is all he is fit for."

" He ought to be dancing on an organ, as you very truly remark; but I will endeavor to find a broader platform from whence to amuse Paris. And he will not dance a waltz, M. Gaillard, nor yet will he indulge his limbs in the graceful movements of the mazurka. He will dance the can-can, will Pierre Pelisson—ahu!"

"You are going to play a practical joke on him?"

"Oh, no! I am only going to make him dance for my amusement; but to do so, I want Prince Toto's address. He is in Paris?"

"He is living at No. 10, Rue de Perpignan," said Gaillard, finishing the champagne. "But I doubt if he will help you."

"I don't want him to," said De Nani, entering the address in his tablets. "I only want the number of the house and the name of the street."

"I ought not to have told you!" cried Gaillard, suddenly remembering his promise to Toto.

"Why not?"

"He made me promise to tell no one where he is living, nor about Célestin."

"Ah, have no fear!" said De Nani, making another entry in his tablets. "Toto will not object to my knowing his address; he knows that I am a safe man, a man to be trusted—ahu, *ventre St. Gris!* Could I tell you, M. Maillard——"

" Gaillard."

" Paillard," continued De Nani, who, now that he had obtained all or nearly all the information he wanted, began to put on frills and forget names. " Could I tell you, M. Paillard, how I love this dear Toto, you might with your genius make from it a little poem; it transcends the love of David for Jonathan, this affection of mine for Toto. He is so joyous, he is so young, he is such a charming host. You remember that delightful dinner where we first made acquaintance; I feel I can never repay Toto for that piece of hospitality. But I will try, as far as in me lies—I will try."

" I tell you what," said Gaillard, putting on his hat and lighting a cigarette: " you would do Toto a great service if you could induce him to leave that wretched hole he is in, and give up art and all that nonsense."

" And Célestin? "

" Yes; she is worse than art. Between you and me, I don't know how he can stand it, living with

an illiterate woman like that; she has not two ideas
in her head. I don't believe she can read, and,
what is worse, I don't believe she wants to. They
do their own cooking. Imagine a man of Toto's
position in the world—faugh! it makes me ill."

This was an untruth—cooking was rarely done
in the atelier of Toto, for Célestin was the worst
cook in the world, excepting perhaps Toto; but it
was true enough for De Nani.

"And this Célestin—what was she before Toto
took her from the mud?"

"She was a hat-maker—she is still. Trims hats
and that sort of thing."

"Whilst Toto paints those delightful pictures of
his?"

"Yes. But the worst is, he cannot sell them,—
I know by his face,—and he is frightfully hard up."

"Soon," said De Nani, with a horrid leer, "our
friend Toto will cast his brushes aside, and live
upon the diligence of this pretty Célestin. It is
what all these artists do when unsuccessful. We
must save him from this."

"I wish you would."

" Before to-morrow evening," said De Nani, " I hope to cure this charming Toto of his fever for fame and his hunger for art. Who is this? Why, it is M. Wolf. I must bid you now good-day, M. Gaillard, as I have some matters of importance to transact with M. Wolf."

Wolf came in, hat in hand and spectacles gleaming, as Gaillard went out. De Nani removed the remains of the *déjeuner* from the table onto the floor, and greeted the newcomer.

" You are just the man I want," said the Marquis. " I have an interview to write, and I want you to assist me. I have all the facts. That is right, take a seat and a pen."

Gaillard went off feeling rather huffed at the summary manner in which De Nani had dismissed him. His hatred of the old man, which had vanished before the champagne and the knowledge of his downfall, returned somewhat. He determined, having nothing better to do, to betake himself to Toto's atelier, and spend the afternoon smoking cigarettes and talking to Célestin about his poems. Célestin made an admirable audience for a minor poet, even although she was an illiterate woman and scarcely knew how to read. She had the power of sympathy, and she listened to Gaillard just as she listened to Dodor and Toto. When Gaillard would spout a sonnet, and then abuse it, declaring that it was too full of color, or too sharp in sound, or destitute of perfume, and that he wished he had never written it, Célestin, raising her eyes from her work, would cry, " Oh, but I am sure it is beautiful. It could not be more beautiful. I seem to see those roses you speak of. And how sad, the roses were unhappy! That seems so dreadful, does it not, Désiré?" And then Toto, if he were busy, would give a grunt, and Gaillard would repeat again the sonnet, and declare that the roses were glad now because Célestin had pitied them.

But she would gladden no roses to-day.

" She has a cold," said Toto, pointing to the closed bedroom door. " She got her feet wet yesterday. How glad I am that you have come!"

He was sitting near the stove, and he rose and put on his hat. Someone had a fit of coughing in the bedroom, and Gaillard stood staring at the tulip manufactured by Garnier as though it were a dragon.

"Surely, my dear Désiré, you have not descended to things like these!" He touched the pot warily with the point of his stick, as if fearful of infection.

"Oh, that!" said Toto carelessly. "It is not mine; it is Célestin's. Do not touch it; she is awfully proud of it. Come out with me; I want to talk to you." In the street Toto took Gaillard's arm. "I am so glad you have come. I am in need of a friend. I am in a state of misery. What shall I do with that girl?"

"Why, has she been troubling you? *Mon Dieu!* Désiré, tell me, what is this?"

"No," said Toto, "she has not been troubling me. I only wish she had, I only wish she had. That woman—pah! she is not a woman, she is an angel."

"So are all women till you find them out. But go on, Désiré. Why all this terrible excitement?"

"Why? My God! it is very easy for you to talk. She loves me. Well, then, what am I to do? I have been nearly mad these last few days, and not a soul to speak to. You don't care. You have been off to the Moulin Rouge and Heaven knows where every night!"

"I swear, Désiré," cried Gaillard, "I have been in a worse condition than you. I have been on the edge of suicide. Moulin Rouge! I have not been to the Moulin Rouge. I took to my bed three days ago to read 'Aucassin and Nicolete' and try to forget that I was alive. I have not eaten— morphia and cigarettes alone have passed my lips during the last forty-eight hours. Then I thought of you; then I came, and for reward I am accused like this! No matter."

"If she were an ordinary girl," said Toto, disregarding Gaillard's fantasies, "I would give her five thousand francs and set her up in business, and there would be an end of it."

"Ah, Désiré! ah, Désiré!" gasped Gaillard, like a man trying to speak in a shower bath. "Can it be that at last you are going to return to us? Can——"

"Call me Toto," cried the Prince. "I hate that

vile name Désiré. I put it on with this foolishness
—this rotten art business. Don't mind me, my
dear fellow; let me rave. I have had no one to talk
to for days but Garnier and Célestin. They do not
understand me."

"Go on, go on," said Gaillard, as if Toto had
swallowed poison and he was urging him to vomit.
"Speak away, it will do you good; relieve your
mind—it will save you perhaps from madness.
Ah, I can understand—I can understand what you
must have suffered, my poor Toto! I have been
through it all myself."

"Come in here," said Toto, stopping at a small
café; "we can sit down and talk."

"Yes, let us enter," said Gaillard. "No, do not
touch absinthe in a place like this; if you wish to
die, choose an easier poison. Beer? Yes, let us
have some beer. And now, Toto, continue your
troubles."

"I have only one trouble," said Toto, "and that
is Célestin."

"Ah, *mon Dieu!* that is a trouble easily got
rid of."

"How?"

"Leave Célestin to me."

"What would you do with her?"

"I?—nothing.   I would simply say, "Mlle. Célestin, M. Désiré has been called away to the death-
bed of an aunt in the country.   She will leave him
her entire fortune if he marries at once and according to her desires.'   Then I would say, 'The girl
upon whom his aunt has fixed——' "

"Oh, rubbish!   I could do that myself.   Do
you think if I wanted to I could not kick Célestin
over in half an hour?   You do not understand.
She is like no one else.   She is like a child.   I cannot hurt her.   She would haunt me forever, she
and that lark.   Oh, why did I ever meet her?   But
for her I would have been back days ago out of this
abominable Rue de Perpignan.   If it had not been
for her, I would never have come here at all.   She
drove me on to this stupidity, I don't know why."

"If," said Gaillard rather stiffly, "you still love
this girl so much——"

"But I don't.   I mean this: I thought I was in
love with her, and, somehow, now everything

seems to have gone to pieces all at once; the pleasure went out of my life all at once. I am lingering
on in this infernal part of the town like a thing with
a broken back. I don't know what I am to do."

" I know," said Gaillard.

" What? "

" Take a little cottage in the country and put
your Célestin there with her lark."

" Yes, I might do that; only I will have to go
there every day or live there."

" In the name of Heaven, why? "

" Because it will break her heart if I leave her.
I tell you you do not know her. She has wound
herself round me."

" Well, unwind her."

" She lives for me—I can see it. I did not know
that there were such women in the world, and, of
course, it is my luck to meet one of them and get
myself in this tangle with her. It is very easy for
you to sip your beer and say ' Unwind her.' Suppose a child were to run up to you and put its arms
round you, could you box its ears? And, besides,
I have wound myself a bit round her. I have an

affection for her, though I am weary of this love business. I do love her as a child, but then one does not want to spend one's life in the nursery."

"Take a little cottage," reiterated Gaillard; "place her in it. We will go down together, you and I, each day for a fortnight. Then we will drop a day by degrees, and wean her, so to speak. It will take you the whole summer. Well, it is an idealistic way of spending the warm weather. We will have a cottage with clematis on the porch, and a garden filled with old-fashioned flowers. There she will, so to speak, gain her legs, and when she is able to run alone, trust her, she will find a playmate."

"The first thing to be done," said Toto thoughtfully, "is to get away from this part of the town before anyone finds out I am here. I do not want this affair advertised all over Paris. You are certain that no one knows about it. You have hinted it to no one?"

"Absolutely certain—no one. You are in Corsica; that is enough."

"Have you seen my mother lately?"

" I dined with her only yesterday."

" Why, I thought you said you had been in bed for the last four days."

" So I have; but I got up yesterday evening and called upon Mme. la Princesse in reply to a summons. She detained me to dinner."

" What did she want? "

" Only to make inquiries as to you."

" And you said? "

" Oh, I said you were progressing charmingly."

" I hope no one else was there? "

" No, we dined *tête-à-tête*."

" Well, I think it is the best thing I can do."

" What? "

" That idea of yours about the country. I could take rooms for a while somewhere. The only thing is, Célestin cannot be moved till this cold is better. Isn't it vile luck? It will mean several days before I can get away from this place."

" Could you not move her in a cab? "

" No, she is not strong, and if she got another cold on top of this one it might kill her."

" Have you given her any medicine? "

" I gave her some lozenges, and Garnier brought her some sugar-candy."

" Who is Garnier? "

" He is a painter."

" Oh, one of these wretched *rapins*. Take my advice, Toto, and have a doctor in; he will cure her more quickly than if she were left alone."

" I wanted to, but she implored me not. She has a horror of doctors and medicine."

" Have you put poultices on her chest? "

" Mercy, no! "

" You ought to poultice her. I frequently suffer from colds in the early spring, and Mme. Plon declares that I would not be alive but for her poultices. It will cut it short. Have you a bronchitis kettle? "

" No; she hasn't got bronchitis; she has only got a cough and a pain in the side."

" No matter; it would stop her from getting bronchitis. You ought also to give her sweet spirits of niter. I assure you, Toto, you never can tell what a cold turns to; and this girl, should she get really ill, may keep her bed for a month, and then where would you be? In cases like this, we ought to act on the principle of the firemen, who play on unconsumed buildings in order to prevent them from catching fire. If I were you, I would insist on a doctor. Well, well, I do not press the point—she is not mine. Let us talk on other things. Have you heard that Pelisson has cut De Nani adrift? No, of course you have not."

"How can I know what is going on in this place?"

"True; but, even so, it only occurred last night. De Nani seems quite resigned, but I would not wonder if he played some trick upon our friend Pelisson. He wanted your address."

"Pelisson?"

"No, De Nani," said Gaillard, who almost bit his tongue for letting this cat out of its bag.

"I hope you did not give it to him."

Gaillard shrugged his shoulders.

"For that old man is my evil star. I do not believe I would have been here now but for his insult that night. You remember? Well, I am going back to the atelier."

"How much money have you left, Toto?"

"I have only five hundred francs."

"You had better let me bring you some more. Give me a check. You have not your check-book? Well, write one out for five hundred francs on a piece of paper, and I will take it and cash it for you, and bring you the money to-morrow."

"You will not turn up again if I let you have all that."

"Toto!"

"I know you so well. See here, what time will you promise to turn up, if I give you my check?"

Gaillard debated with himself.

"I will be at your atelier at one o'clock, punctually."

"You promise?"

"I promise."

CHAPTER II.

THE STORY OF FANTOFF AND BASTICHE.

THEY went back to the atelier, and Toto, who had not breakfasted, got together some wine and bread and cold stewed beef. Gaillard sat down to table also, to keep him company. Then the poet ventured into the bedroom to talk to the sick girl and cheer her up.

Célestin was lying on her side, facing the door, with very bright eyes and flushed cheeks. On the wall over the bed hung a colored print of our Lord Jesus carrying a lamb; she had brought it with her from her room near the Rue de Babylone. An orange lay on the quilt, one of six brought by Garnier that morning; she had eaten the other five and swallowed the pulp, an act which would have caused a physician to shudder. On a rush-bottomed chair near by lay the lozenges given to her by Mme. Liard,—redoubtable lozenges, according to the label on the box,—also the sugar candy of Garnier.

Gaillard sat down beside the bed; he took the sick girl's hand, and, stroking it like a mother, called her his *pauvre petite* Célestin. She quite touched his heart—her sickness, her pitiable air of helplessness; the orange on the quilt, and the picture of the Lord Jesus watching over her.

She had been in great pain all the morning,—a cruel pain, like a hot-iron, in her right lung,—but she was better of the pain now and the cough; she told him so in a mutter, and then asked for a fairy tale.

Toto looked in, munching a biscuit; he nodded his head as if satisfied and withdrew, whilst Gaillard in a fit of genius improvised a fairy tale. It was about a green giant called Fantoff. He was quite green, his hair was grass, and his feet were like roots uprooted in some terrible upheaval; his fingers were like carrots, and he turned brown every autumn with the leaves, the larks in spring mistaking his head for a field built on it; so that in this happy season of the year wherever he walked larks sang above him, and whenever he scratched his head a dozen nests were destroyed. At this Cé-lestin, with Dodor in her mind, said "No, no." So the poet passed on to the cat Mizar and the dwarf Blizzard, whom the giant had, one day in a fit of idleness, carved from a forked carrot; and Célestin, remembering Garnier's tulip, believed that this might possibly be true.

Blizzard, forgetful of the debt of creation, dared to fall in love with the lady beloved by Fantoff, whose name was Primavera, and whose abode was the Castle of Flowers. A hundred thousand tulips defended this castle from behind a holly hedge. They were divided into five armies—red, white, yellow, chocolate, and striped; and Célestin in a half-dream beheld the valiant host whilst Gaillard rambled on.

The gardener generalissimo of this army was blind,—he had been blinded by the beauty of Primavera,—and one day as he was wheeling back to the castle a barrow full of roses, who had gone out to fight the camellias and had been badly beaten, Blizzard the dwarf slipped into it under the roses, intent on gaining an entrance to the castle at all hazards, there to declare his love. What happened? Simply this: Algebar, the bird of Paradise, flapped its sapphire wings and shrieked out, "Beware! A carrot is trying to enter the Castle of Flowers. Beware, beware!" and before the faithful bird could call it thrice the door opened, and out came Bastiche, the porter.

Bastiche was a giant, who had once been a clothes basket; he was seven hundred feet high, and creaked as he walked. Primavera in a fit of foolishness had endowed him with life, and as he stood on the castle steps he opened his lid and shut it again. He also quite forgot the warning of Algebar, for at that moment rose up from behind the holly hedge the great green head of Fantoff, the larks singing above it merrily.

Fantoff, be it observed, was quite unconscious of the scheme of Blizzard. He had determined to raid the castle that day on his own account, just as Blizzard had determined to sneak in. Well, listen. There stood Fantoff in all his glory. The tulips shuddered at the sight, and the blind gardener put down his barrow, for he felt in some manner that something was about to happen; and there stood Bastiche, creaking with anger, whilst little Blizzard in the barrow shook the dead roses with laughter. Fantoff and Bastiche stared at each other, Fantoff with derision, Bastiche with envy and hate, whilst Algebar flew through the garden and screamed.

Bastiche, then, as if oblivious of the presence of a foe, gazed up at the clouds and sniffed, and asked the sky where could the smell of manure be coming from; whilst Fantoff inquired of the tulips whether this was the washing-day at the castle? This allusion to his birth quite upset the calm of Bastiche, who descended the steps, opened the garden gate, and like a fool left the protection of the tulip army and holly hedge.

Then, on the plain before the Castle of Flowers, ensued a battle such as never before was witnessed in Fairyland. The mushrooms formed a ring seven miles in diameter, and in this ring the heroes struggled; the sound filled the air for many miles, mixed with the sounds of many things hastening to see the fight. At the end of an hour the plain was

strewn with unwashed clothes, and the battle was
with Fantoff. He tore the lid off Bastiche, and,
not content with this, what must he do but insert
his great green head into the yawning opening, to
tear the heart of his enemy out with his teeth. But
Bastiche had no heart, and here lies one of the
morals of the story. For Fantoff had no knowledge of anatomy and he did not know the impossi-
bility of slaying a man without a heart—a critic for
instance, or a Bastiche. What did he do? Burrowing deeper and deeper to find his heart, he got
his shoulders implicated in the creaking body of
Bastiche, and burrowing deeper still he was implicated to the loins.

" He creaks," cried Fantoff, " so he is still
alive! " and went deeper till he was in to the knees.
Then he found that he could not get out, for
Bastiche had in death taken upon him the revenge
of a clothes basket. The fairies tried to pull him
out, and also the cat Mizar, but it was of no avail;
so they wheeled him away, and the cat Mizar followed to the grave.

In the Castle of Flowers the Lady Primavera

turned from watching the fight and its miserable conclusion; she saw an object at her feet. It was Blizzard the dwarf; he had left the barrow during the fight, and, entering the castle by the scullery door, sneaked upstairs, and now upon one knee was declaring his love; and she returned his passion, it seems. But their bliss was of short duration. For one day, chancing to fall asleep in the kitchen, the cook, who was short of vegetables, cut him up and put him in the pot, and the Lady Primavera ate him in her soup, and so there was an end of Blizzard.

For Fantoff read genius; Primavera, fame; Bastiche, the spiteful critics; Blizzard, the popular author, whose books sell by the ton; Mizar, the faithful few. The story also as told by Gaillard had several immoral meanings quite Greek to Célestin. It was, in fact, the work of Papillard, for the downfall of De Nani had thawed that humorist in his cell.

"That is all," said Gaillard. "To-morrow, if you are better, I will tell you of the adventures of the cat Mizar, and of all that happened when he

saw his reflection in the looking-glass of the wizard
Fantoum.   Fantoum had a blue face; he was half-
brother to Fantoff, and his enemy was the giant
Boum-Boum, whose children under the spell of the
wizard were turned into drums before the age of
twenty; that is to say, the boys—the girls turned
into drumsticks.   I will tell you a story each day,
my little Célestin, and then we will print them all
in a pretty volume bound in butterfly-blue vellum,
and call them ' Tales Told to Célestin.'   With the
money from its sale we will buy a cottage at Montmorency and keep bees; we will support ourselves
on bees and fairy tales.   And now I must say
adieu, and run away until to-morrow."

"Ah, Montmorency!" murmured Célestin, as
Gaillard's high collar and frock-coat vanished and
the door closed on them, leaving her alone.

Toto gave the poet his check, imploring him to
wait a little longer and keep him company.

But Gaillard had now the check in his pocket,
and the vision of Pleasure was kicking her skirts
before his eyes, a box of cigars in one hand, a bottle
of champagne in the other.   So he took the oppor-

tunity of Garnier's entrance to make his exit, swearing to return on the morrow at noon, and ran down the Rue de Perpignan, making for the right side of the Seine just as a thirsty animal makes for water.

Then Garnier, like the poet, came in to see the patient; his pockets were bulging with things, and he held in his hands a square paper parcel; it was a little picture he had painted for Célestin—a droll little picture of a Cupid with a cold, an ominous little picture, perhaps, for, as Gaillard truly said, who can tell what a cold may turn to?

CHAPTER III.

THE REVENGE OF M. DE NANI.

THAT night Célestin, it would seem, grew worse. Toto, who had made his bed on the couch in the atelier, slept so soundly that he did not hear her delirious and rambling conversation.

Gaillard's fairy people visited her, and Bastiche and Fantoff commanded her terrified attention as they did battle once more on the greensward in front of the Castle of Flowers, whilst Fantoum watched them across the holly hedge. Then the battle scene vanished, and Mizar the cat came and took his seat upon her chest. His eyes were pale blue, and flickered like spirit lamps in a draught; she implored of him to give her water to drink, and for answer he changed into Gaillard.

Through all these fancies ran the form of an old man. It was De Nani, whom she had seen once for a moment as he talked to Toto at the Gare du

Nord: his lascivious and painted face peeped at her here and there from behind hedges and trees in this phantom land, whilst over all flew Algebar, the paradisiacal bird, rending the attenuated air with the constant mournful cry, " Beware! beware! A carrot is trying to enter the Castle of Flowers."

With daylight all these strange fancies vanished, and at seven o'clock, when Toto entered her room to inquire how she felt, she answered that she was quite well, but had been dreaming terrible things. She implored him in her husky whisper to bring in Dodor, and having placed the cage close to the bed and removed the green cover, he made some coffee and brought her some with half a buttered roll.

She drank the coffee, and when he was gone she hid the buttered roll so that he might think she had eaten it. At all hazards she must keep up the appearance of not being " very bad," for if Toto were alarmed he would, without doubt, send for a doctor, and that meant spending money. Fully five hundred times had Mme. Liard recounted to her the frightful expense M. Liard had put her to in his last illness; she always spoke of the doctor's bill with hands outstretched a yard wide.

" Pills—a little box not bigger than a thimble, three francs—three francs, as I am an honest woman! and plasters a yard wide that did nothing, as far as I could see, but put the good man in pain; and not only plasters, but bottles of stuff, sometimes twice a day, red and brown and yellow, and always changing till one grew giddy; and then when he had killed him wanted to cut him open to see what he died of. May I never reach heaven if I tell a lie! That is what doctors are!"

No wonder Célestin dreaded the craft, and much preferred Choiseul's lozenges and Garnier's sugar candy to the ruinous bottles and the pills at three francs a thimbleful, and the chance of being cut open " to see what she died of."

Cough lozenges and sugar candy are not perhaps the most effective remedies for acute pneumonia, especially when the patient has only one lung; but perhaps, taking that fact into consideration, they were as serviceable as any others.

At nine o'clock the concierge, a stolid woman,

deaf as a stone, came up to settle the bedroom and see to the patient. She brought up with her a newspaper that had just been left in by a little boy. The wrapper was addressed in a crabbed hand to " M. Cammora, No. 10, Rue de Perpignan," and Toto wondered whose the handwriting could be, for he had never seen the scrawl of M. le Marquis de Nani.

It was a copy of that morning's *Pantin.* The first page was occupied with foreign news and a heavy leading article by Pelisson on the prospects of beet sugar turning foreign sugars out of the market, and ending with a regret that the Minister of Agriculture had let several chances slip for the betterment of the prospects of France.

Toto turned to the second page and came upon a long article marked with pencil. He thought at the first glance that it was the review of a novel, for it was headed " Painter and Prince." Then after six lines he discovered it was an interview, after twelve lines that it was an interview with himself.

The interviewer, it seems, had discovered that a

certain illustrious young Prince whom the whole world had imagined to be in Corsica stalking the nimble moufflon, was in fact in Paris, stalking art —working, in fact, like any child of the people in an attic, Rue de Perpignan, No. 10. And as Toto saw his address thus publicly proclaimed the hair of his head stood on end.

The interview was written in Wolf's chatty manner. Wolf had three manners: the worshipful manner, which he applied to geniuses, great statesmen, and successful tradesmen, when those gentry fell into his hands; the cut-and-dried, for strike leaders, members of the chamber, people whose houses had caught fire suspiciously; and the chatty, for actresses, successful clowns, prominent divorcees, etc. The chatty interview generally began on the stairs, with a short description of first impressions.

The stairs of Toto's house, it seems, gave one the impression of abject poverty.

"When we reached the first floor," said this mouthpiece of De Nani, "we inquired of a charwoman for the young Prince ——. She declared her ignorance of such a person, no Prince to her knowledge having ever inhabited the house.

" The interviewer, thus left to his own resources, pursued his quest through this frightful house, which recalled nothing so much as the Maison Corbeau of Victor Hugo. On the fourth floor, a hissing sound rewarded his ear, and knocking at a door, a well-known voice desired him to enter. Here he found a picture that would have gladdened the heart of Jean Jacques Rousseau.

" By the window of a poverty-stricken room sat a girl trimming hats—a girl of the people, exquisitely pretty, and possessing that innate refinement common to all Parisiennes, no matter how humble their origin. By the little stove stood a handsome young man, preparing the modest meal they were evidently to share together.

" It was the Prince, who laughed joyously, and placed the little pan upon the floor, whilst he shook the interviewer warmly by the hand."

The whole thing had a most horribly actual air. The teeming brain of Wolf had supplied little details impossible, one would say, to be false. The foolish lovers who had renounced, one her home, the other his world, for the sake of art and love in an attic, stood before one in the flesh. Wolf, inspired by champagne and the dictation of his editor, had worked with the fervor and insight of a poet; and one almost wept over the struggling pair, till one remembered that the Prince was worth half a million of money, and then one laughed till one's sides ached.

"We are very happy," said the Prince, at the conclusion of this weird interview. "Tell all my friends to come and see me, now that you have found me out. Tell them also that there is only one true happiness—to be young and poor, and mated to the woman one loves."

"That last line," had murmured De Nani to himself, "will, I have no doubt, vastly amuse Mme. la Princesse and Mlle. Powhair."

Toto let *Pantin* drop, and turned his white face to the window, as if he expected to see all Paris looking in and laughing. He knew, as indeed was the fact, that men were tumbling out of bed bursting with laughter, and running into their wives' bedrooms *Pantin* in hand; that starch-faced valets were shaking under their starch, as they handed *Pantin* to their masters on silver salvers with cups of chocolate; that young De Harnac, who was more English than his own bulldog, was crying " My Gawd! " and kicking his legs about in bed with delight as he read *Pantin;* that Mme. la Princesse was prostrated, and Mlle. Powhair—he could not imagine what Helen Powers was saying or thinking. The thought of her was somehow the worst part of all this trouble.

His lips were dry, and they felt as if they never could become moist again. He was quite calm, but this calmness of Toto's would have frightened his mother to behold. He neither shrieked nor tore his hair; but, indeed, the latter feat would have been impossible, for a fortnight ago he had had it cropped to the bone in imitation of Garnier.

The hilt of this dagger was the ingratitude of Pelisson, Gaillard & Co.—the men who had been his guests, to whom he had lent money, and who had now stabbed him in this cruel manner before

all Paris.   Little did he know of the raving Pelisson, who, having sought vainly for Froissart, had
returned by the night mail, which stops at Amiens
and arrives in Paris at seven in the morning, only
to find this horrible snake curled in *Pantin*.   Pelisson at this moment was dragging the terrified Gaillard out of bed, who was protesting that he knew
nothing of the matter, just as Scribe ten minutes
ago had protested that eighteen thousand francs
were missing from the safe, he could not tell how;
and as Saxe, the German foreman, had declared
that the usual big edition of *Pantin* was out, and
could not be got back, not if God came out of Himmel, and that it was not Saxe's fault that this
schweinhund article had crawled into print—whilst
Struve, whose practical joke had long ago laid the
seeds of all this mischief, was the only man uncon-
cerned by it as he lay asleep after a hard night's
work, and dreaming of stained-glass windows and
saints who had strayed into art.

But Toto knew nothing of all this: he thought
this cruel and spiteful trick the work of his friends.
He had always liked Pelisson, and he had liked

Gaillard.   Gaillard had been, in fact, a kind of necessity to him—a sort of dry-nurse, who wiped his
nose and said " There, there!" when he was fret-
ful, and listened to his secrets, and told him tales,
and put him up to resist his mother.

A man of the world would have seen at once that
some trick had been played on *Pantin.*   Pelisson,
of all men in the world, was the last to let such an
article appear in his paper; especially as it was leveled against a man who was virtually part proprietor.   Gaillard, too, was entirely out of court.   But
Toto was not a man of the world, and the bitterest
thing to him in this severe humiliation was the supposed authorship.

He took up *Pantin,* folded it, and hid it under
one of the cushions of the couch.   The act, performed on the impulse of a moment, revealed to
him in a dramatic manner his position.   Of what
use was the hiding of one copy of *Pantin* under a
cushion when fifty thousand *Pantins* were bellow-
ing his shame all over Paris?   So he snatched it
out and flung it open on the table as if for everyone
to read—a useless act, for everyone was reading it.

Then he smoked a cigarette. In an hour of semi-delirium he smoked ten. The thing was so immensely vile, so wanton, such bad form, that the very enormity of it calmed him. A man who learns that the bank has smashed, that his wife has eloped, and that his house is burnt to the ground all at the same moment, ten to one receives the news with calmness—the blow stuns him. He feels that Fate and Death and other heroic personages have condescended to turn their undivided attention for a moment to his affairs—he is almost a hero, in fact.

So Toto turned from blank horror to the heroic mood. The whole world was against him; well, he would stick to his guns. He almost felt glad that all this had happened, and lit another cigarette just as Garnier entered, bearing in his hand a huge bunch of black grapes for Célestin. They were muscatels, and must have cost him a little fortune, unless he stole them, or, what is more probable, obtained them on credit.

"Garnier," said Toto, his cheeks flushing slightly, "see here," and he pointed his cigarette with a wave at *Pantin* lying open on the table.

" And she? " asked Garnier, as he made a sign towards the closed door of Célestin's room, laying his grapes down on the table and taking up the paper all at the same time.

" She is better."

" Ah, this which is marked with crosses? "

" Yes, read it."

Garnier began to read, standing under the top-light and holding the paper at full length before him. In a moment he folded the sheet in a more comfortable manner and continued reading calmly and without any sign of astonishment. At one place he frowned slightly, where Célestin's name appeared, then when he had finished he laid *Pantin* back on the table beside the grapes.

" Well? " inquired Toto.

" I do not think that is in very good taste," said Garnier dryly.

" What! is that all you have to say—not in very good taste? "

" My friend," said Garnier, " it is no affair of

mine; but it makes my fingers tingle none the less. Were it an affair of mine, I would make you eat that journal and all it contains—*vé!* I have spoken."

"Ah, stupid!" cried Toto, uncrossing his legs and moving his arms about. "You think *I* have written that!" and the corners of his mouth went up in a very mirthless rictus.

"But surely——"

"I? Why, cannot you see that it is a hoax? No one came here to see me—I was not frying things over the stove. Do you think for a moment I would expose myself like that, and give my address? It was done to make fun of me—everyone will be laughing at me. Can't you see?"

"Oh, my friend," said Garnier, "forgive me, forgive me! How could I have been so stupid and so blind? Ah, owl that you are!" and he gave his great chest a thump with his great fist, and then came to the couch and sat by Toto, and rested his hand on his knee, and poured out consolation in the language of Arles, punctuated with explosive oaths.

" Oh, it does not matter. Do you think that I care? I do in a way, for it shows me the villainy of the world."

" Ah, you are right; this villain of a world—it is a beast! But *tenez!* my dear friend, I hear the little Célestin coughing. I will give her a grape."

He ran into Célestin's room with the bunch of grapes, and Toto heard his voice murmuring to her, mixed with Dodor's voice trying over a few bars of a song in a despondent sort of manner; for Célestin's illness seemed to have put him out of heart during the last couple of days. Then Garnier came back, closing the door softly behind him, and raising up his hands at Célestin's weakness.

" Say, my dear friend," said Garnier, " do you not think a doctor ought to see her? As for me, I do not believe in them, but still—but still——"

He stopped speaking, and followed the direction of Toto's frozen stare.

At the door of the atelier, just pushed open, appeared the semi-hysterical figure of Gaillard, his hat tilted back, his long frock-coat hanging loose, and his necktie hastily put on. He had evidently dressed in a hurry, for he wore odd boots—one patent leather and the other plain kid.

" Do you see that man? " said Toto, clutching Garnier's arm. " Do you see that man? "

" *Mais oui.* "

" Then you see the biggest scoundrel in Paris," said Toto, and he struck a match and lit a cigarette to show his coolness, averting his eyes at the same time from the apparition at the door.

Gaillard raised up his two hands like one of Struve's stained-glass saints, and then dropped them with a flop. He did not cross the threshold, for he was perhaps afraid of being kicked out.

" Do not be afraid to come in," said Toto; " I will not assault you. I am too utterly lost in admiration of your charming insolence—it is a masterpiece."

" Afraid! " said Gaillard, coming in very slowly. " Afraid—afraid of what? I have no fear left; Toto, Désiré, my friend, we are all ruined. Pelisson is in despair; Wolf is committing suicide—I saw him myself being held down by four men. That villain—that villain—that villain of a De

Nani, the cause of it all, has vanished. All the money is gone from the safe; Scribe is in a state of dementia. I escape from this inferno and rush to you for sympathy, and I am greeted as a scoundrel!"

"What do I care about De Nani?" inquired Toto. "Look at that."

"Yes," said Gaillard, "look at that; but I have no need to look at that—it is burnt into my brain. I could have slain Wolf with my two hands when he confessed an hour ago, but, *ma foi!* he was too much slain already; besides, it was not his fault. Whose fault? Why, De Nani's. Pelisson left him in charge; did I not tell you so yesterday?"

"De Nani?"

"Yes. Wolf has confessed he wrote the article under the inspiration of that scoundrel. The old man dictated it word for word; it was a parting shot at Pelisson. My back feels broken. Why, who is this?"

A sound of cackling laughter came from outside, and the foolish and foppish form of young De Harnac appeared at the door, followed by the figure of Valfray, his little black mustache twisted up at the ends and his eyeglass in his eye.

They saw Toto seated on the chintz-covered couch beside Gaillard, a momentary vision ere they found themselves being led like two naughty children across the dusty landing towards the stairs by a huge man with a Provençal accent.

"It is not good to laugh at one's friends when they are in trouble," said Garnier in his large way, and with a perfume of garlic. "You will go, please, immediately, and call another day. These are the stairs—yes, *if* you please."

"Oh, what have you done?" said Toto, when he came back. "Those two fools will run all over Paris telling lies about me now—no matter! Gaillard, my dear friend, come with me into the street; I must speak to you alone. Garnier, my friend, you will see to Célestin till I return, will you not?"

He ran into her room for a moment. She tried to hold up her arms to him, and he kissed her, but he did not see her face; her sunken eyes, the blueness of her lips, all those signs which spoke of that terrible pneumonia which kills like the dagger of an unskillful assassin—with great pain, but none the less surely.   He saw only the smooth head of De Harnac, the black mustache and glittering monocle of Valfray, and the broad back of Garnier interposing.

"I am going out for a little; I will not be long, and Garnier will see that you want nothing till my return."

"Oh, Désiré, do not leave me!   I am very ill—not so very ill, but still——   Oh, what will become of you should I die—and Dodor?   Is he in the cage?   I have not heard him move."

"I will be back soon," said Toto, "and Dodor is all right."

"But I have not heard him move."

He lifted the parrot cage, and held it up to show that the bird was safe, and Dodor spread his wings like a little eagle, as if indignant that anyone should touch his house but Célestin.   She glanced at him as if satisfied.

"Does it rain?"

"No."

"I hear the sound of rain—do not get wet. You will return?"

"Very soon."

He did not know what he was saying; it was like a conversation in a dream. Then he left her and took his hat, and left the atelier leaning on Gaillard's arm, whilst Garnier sat on the couch and mused.

"I must leave Paris at once—I must leave Paris at once!" burst out Toto when they were in the Rue de Perpignan. "I must leave it forever; nothing like this ever happened to anyone before. My God! I am going mad. It is like one of those dreams when we seem to be walking about the streets naked. Did you see that fool De Harnac's face, and Valfray looking all round with his eye-glass?"

"It is all dreadful," said Gaillard. "Let us, for Heaven's sake, sit down somewhere and think—let us, in the name of Heaven, get some brandy somewhere. I was drunk last night,—I confess it without shame,—and my nerves are in pieces. Look at my hand—is that the hand of a person who ought to be troubled? Suppose a fit were to overtake me? Well, then—yes, let us leave Paris. Oh, my God, I have odd boots on! Did you see that woman?—she laughed at them. I must have been absolutely insane all this morning not to have noticed them before. I have been walking about all the morning like this."

"Yes, I must leave Paris at once. Come in here and sit down. *Garçon*, brandy, a decanter, and some Apollinaris water."

"It is the first warning—I knew it was coming; ataxia always begins like this. My dear Toto, you know nothing about it; I have read the whole subject up in the Bibliothèque Nationale. It begins with forgetfulness in little things; one finds one's self walking down the street in slippers, or forgetting how to spell one's name, and one dies like a raving maniac. Then, one has tremor of the hand —look at my hand."

"Drink some brandy," said Toto, rousing up a bit from his own misery. "You will be all right; I have often been like that myself."

"No matter; if I die, Pelisson will have killed

me. He burst into my room absolutely like a
tiger; you can fancy the shock to one in my condition. I was absolutely dragged from my
bed—threatened with violence if I did not
divulge all that I knew about this infamous
article."

"Don't *speak* of it!" cried Toto, "don't, don't!
I want to get to some quiet place where I know no
one. Come, I am going to Struve's rooms; I must
see him and ask him to take some money to this
girl. I will write you a check at his rooms and
you can go and cash it; then I will go to some
country place. You will come with me, will you
not? You are the only friend I have."

"To the ends of the earth," answered Gaillard.
"This brandy has saved my reason if not my
life; I will finish what is in the little decanter if you
will not."

He finished the brandy, and then, rising, took
Toto's arm.

It was half-past eleven now, and the day promised to be very warm—a perfect summer's day with
scarcely a breeze or cloud. The narrow street was

black in the shadow, gold in the sunshine, and a barrel-organ was playing " Santa Lucia."

" Yes, I am better now; the world is not so distinctly horrible as it was a moment ago. But, Toto, if you are intent on going to Struve's rooms, how are we to get there? We are sure to meet people we know."

" We must take a carriage. Curse it! I wish it were winter; there are no closed carriages. You can get a brougham to take me to the station when we reach Struve's, but how are we to get there? I can't parade myself before Paris. I know,—it is the only thing we can do,—we will take an omnibus from the Boul' Miche. We shall meet no one that we know in an omnibus."

In the Boul' Miche they were fortunate enough to find an omnibus just stopped and disgorging some passengers—one, moreover, that would drop them actually at Struve's door; but they had to wait whilst three other passengers got in before them. There was a girl in a summer hat that would have brought tears to Celestin's eyes, a priest, and a fat lady bearing a lobster tied to a

string; then they found that there was only one inside place left.

"You must go outside," said Toto.

"But, Désiré, think for a moment. I cannot
possibly do this; everyone will see me. Let us
wait and take the next."

"Struve may be out if we delay," said Toto, getting into the vehicle wearily, and, as it was starting,
Gaillard was forced to mount on the outside, where
he sat with his handkerchief to his face as if his nose
were bleeding and his hat tilted over his eyes.
Fortunately, no one saw him, though he imagined
in his agony that all Paris was watching him from
the sky, the housetops, the windows, and the street.

Struve was at breakfast. He had evidently been
reading *Pantin*, for it was open before him, and he
put a dish of kidneys over the damnable article in a
pathetic attempt to hide it as the poet and the
painter entered his room, with all the dejection of
a couple of cats that have just been washed.

"We are going away," said Gaillard.

"Sit down," lisped Struve, jumping up. "Toto,
I am very glad to see you—have a cigar, have a

cigarette? Now what is all this nonsense I have heard? Gaillard, for goodness' sake put your head straight; you are not a lily. Pelisson has been here—I know all this cursed nonsense; he has been let in by old De Nani. I always told him he would; everyone is cursing poor old Pelisson for a fool. Well, then, what matter? it will soon blow over."

"We are going away," said Toto, taking up Gaillard's whine; "at least, I am—forever!"

"So," said Struve, lighting a cigarette, "you are going away forever; and when are you coming back? Toto, for goodness' sake, don't think that I am joking. I know what Paris is, and for Heaven's sake don't go about with that long face! Laugh, laugh, and you are clad in triple brass; no one ever laughs at a man who is laughing—they always laugh with him. Laugh at Pelisson, laugh at De Nani, do as they do at the carnival ball; a jester strikes me with his bauble, I strike Jules, Jules Alphonse, and so it goes on. Don't take this thing seriously."

"I cannot laugh," said Toto, looking at his boots with the air of a martyr.

" Well, then, smoke."

" Thanks, yes, I will take a cigarette. I want to speak to you; but first I want Auguste to do something for me."

He sat down at the writing table and made out a holograph check for ten thousand francs, and dispatched Gaillard with it to the bank.

" Go to Porcheron's and get a brougham, and come back in it, my dear fellow."

" But your luggage? "

" Oh, I will buy things wherever I go."

Gaillard departed, and Toto resumed his seat.

" I want to tell you all," he said. " There is a girl; she brought this mischief upon me, though it was not entirely her fault."

" Oh, these girls! " murmured Struve.

" I know they are frightful, but, still, I must do something for this girl."

" Pah! Give her five hundred francs—I know what girls are—and forget her."

" Oh, for the matter of that, she is not—she loves me, I think, in her way—of course she does not know all the mischief she has done: how could she? No matter. I want you to call this afternoon and explain that I am gone away for a while."

"I say, you know," said Struve, who did not relish the idea of acting as ambassador between Toto and some hussy, who would probably pull his hair for his pains, "would it not be better for you to write? There is something much more final about a letter left in by a postman than a message taken by a friend."

"I could not write to her, and I want you to give her some money. Gaillard is bringing ten thousand francs back; I will give her three. Of course I will provide for her afterwards. Do, my dear fellow, help me in this, and I will be forever grateful; besides, you will never see me again."

"All right," said Struve; "I will do as you ask."

The three thousand francs decided him. There were few women of this kind who would pull the hair of a messenger armed with the consolation of a three-thousand-franc note; besides, he felt a sympathy for the unfortunate Toto, this sparrow who had built too high. They sat for half an hour smoking.

"Of course," said Toto, "the affair does not end here between De Nani and me. When I have time to breathe I will find him out."

"What for?"

"To make him fight."

The idea of a duel between Toto and De Nani was almost too much for Struve's gravity. However, he did not laugh.

"You will not find De Nani; he has vanished. Pelisson says the safe has been cleaned out. It was that fool Scribe, the cashier; he lent De Nani the keys for a moment the day before yesterday, and the old fellow must have taken an impression of them in wax. The worst of it is, Pelisson cannot prosecute—the old fellow knows too much about the inner workings of *Pantin*. And yet Pelisson always thought him a fool. No, you will not find De Nani; and if you did, he would not fight. It is my impression that he is a very deep card, this Marquis. You see, Pelisson thought him only a drunken old man who would be wax in his hands. Who is this? "

Gaillard appeared.

" I have a brougham at the door," said Gaillard in a mournful voice, " and here is the money, dear Toto, partly in notes, partly in gold."

MEANWHILE, Garnier, left alone in the atelier, sat musing on the strangeness of things, and waiting for Toto's return. Ten minutes passed by, and half an hour. Through the top-light, which was pulled a bit open, he could hear the sparrows bickering on the roof, and the voice of a hawker in the Rue de Perpignan crying " Strawberries! " whilst a broad dash of sunlight, falling upon the lower part of the wall opposite to him, lit the place with an effulgence of its own, like a great lamp radiating sunbeams.

It seemed such a pity that Célestin should be ill this glorious weather. Presently he heard her voice calling for Désiré in a muffled manner.

" He will be back very soon, my little Célestin," said Garnier, as he stood beside the bed, smiling down upon the patient. " *Mon Dieu!* my poor child, how blue your lips have become, even within so short a time. Say to me, Célestin, how you feel."

"I feel choking," murmured Célestin, with a terrible look of appeal, as though she had but that moment recognized the extent of her illness with the fact that Toto had gone out.

Garnier made a little dramatic back-step, which he corrected by folding his hands loosely in front of him and rubbing them slightly one upon the other as if nothing was the matter. The frightful truth suddenly broke upon him that Célestin, his little Célestin, was terribly ill.

"I feel choking—it is terrible—my friend."

"Oh, yes," said Garnier, dropping beside her on his knees. "What is it? You frighten me. Have you pain? Speak, Célestin, and tell me."

"Oh, no pain, but I cannot breathe. Stay, I am better now—the weight has gone a bit; but it will come back. I am afraid to die; what will he do? I would have worked for him; but it is no use—I cannot if I am dead. And he was in trouble; I could see it on his face. We are so poor, you know."

Garnier felt horrified, paralyzed in the knees and unable to move.

"What is this you say? what is this you say?" he murmured.

"Is it raining?"

"Oh, no, it is very fine.   What is this I hear you say, Célestin?   Are you very ill?   It is bright sunshine outside; there is no rain."

"I hear the sound of rain."

"It does not rain," said Garnier in a heartbroken voice as he watched her eyes wandering about the room as if pursuing some fugitive vision. "Can you not see the sun shining at the window?"

Célestin sighed.

"Désiré has gone out.   When did he go?   Ah, yes, I remember now; he would not be a moment, he said."

"He will not be a moment," said Garnier, stumbling to his feet.   "I will run and see if I can fetch him.   I will not be absent one little moment."

He stole out of the bedroom, through the atelier, and rushed down the stairs, hatless and as if the top of the house were on fire.   There was, fortunately, a doctor in the street; he lived but a few doors away, and by good luck had just returned from his round of morning visits.

He was a depressed-looking young man with a pointed beard, somewhat like Gaillard in face, but not nearly so well dressed. He came at once with Garnier, and as he took his seat beside Célestin he laid his polished silk hat, crown downwards, upon the floor.

Garnier stood at the end of the bed looking on. He suddenly felt a strong belief in doctors. Dr. Fénélon seemed to him a god; his manner was so assured, and he had the air of one who knew, coupled with the gravity of a judge. He noticed that the doctor wore a bone stud in his white shirt front, and every little detail of his dress, to the patent-leather toecaps of his dull kid boots.

The doctor spoke to Célestin, just a few words by way of introducing himself, and then drew out a watch to assist him in feeling her pulse. The watch had a large spider hand which went hopping along, making sixty hops to the minute. This spider hand deepened Garnier's confidence, as did the binaural stethoscope which the doctor drew out of his breast pocket and swung about his neck.

Garnier turned his face away whilst the physician unbuttoned Célestin's nightdress at the neck. A moment he paused, as if undecided as to stripping her to the waist, Hôtel Dieu fashion, then shook his head, and, slipping the ear-pieces in his ears, began his auscultation.

Garnier, standing with his face averted, heard the sparrows on the roof and an occasional pr-rt, pr-rt from Dodor's cage, as the lark changed his perch, also a piano-organ, the thinnest of sounds fluctuating on the faint breeze blowing from the direction of the Seine.

Sometimes Dr. Fénélon cleared his throat, or said " Pardon." Then he began to percuss, and the little blows sounded as if against something solid.

Garnier turned; the examination was over, and the doctor, the stethoscope swinging still from his neck, was buttoning the top button of the night-dress. This accomplished, he stood just for a second with hands folded, overlooking the patient

from head to feet; one might almost have imagined him measuring her with his eye.

Célestin, whose eyes had been half closed, suddenly opened them, and muttered something in an
alarmed manner.

" What is it? "

" Fantoum," she muttered, shrinking slightly as
if from some vision in the air.

The doctor led Garnier into the atelier, and by
the way he closed the bedroom door Garnier knew
that it was all up.

" Your wife? " asked the doctor, removing the
instrument from his neck and placing it folded in
his breast-pocket.   •

" Oh, no, the wife of a friend—simply that. Ah,
my God! I fear she is worse than we thought."

" So then I can speak: she is moribund. I can
absolutely do nothing. You understand? What
can I do? One lung is gone. Well, then, the
other is greatly touched at the apex—absolutely
solid with pneumonia at the base. She is living by
a piece of lung not so large as my hand. We cannot change all that."

" Can nothing be done? "

" My dear friend, she is to all intents and pur-
poses dead. She has been dying some time—
probably since yesterday."

" Ah, I hear you say all that; you say she is dead.
I have never heard a thing like that before so
frightful. I have heard of doctors keeping people
alive. Well, then, look: it is not the question of
payment; it is not a question of one, two, three napoleons, but thousands! You are not speaking to
a fool; I am a great painter. I have only to close
my hands on the money, and half of what I earn is
yours. I am Gustave Garnier; I never told a lie.
Ask Melmenotte what I can do."

" My dear friend," sighed Dr. Fénélon, " I would
save her for nothing, but I am not God."

" Nothing can be done? "

" Nothing."

" Brandy? "

" I would not trouble her with brandy—it might
even put the flame out; she is just trembling; " and
he held out his hand, imitating the motion of a butterfly poised.

" How long? "

" Perhaps not for hours, possibly a day; perhaps in half an hour—a few minutes.   Were she to sit up in bed, she would expire as if shot."

" Ah, well, we must face it.   You will come in again?   Oh, my God! "

" I will come in this evening.   My dear child," continued the doctor, taking the great arm of Garnier in his thin hand, " I would stay if I could be of use; I can only leave her to you.   No, I would not trouble her with a priest; she is, I am afraid, delirious."

Garnier returned to the bedroom, a look of terrible perplexity on his face.   He could•not grasp the facts.   Full of life and strength, he had never troubled to think of death, it was all so remote; and here it was grasping Célestin.

She was semi-conscious again, and the one word kept repeating itself on her lips, " Désiré, Désiré! " It was like a person crying for water.

" Oh, why does he not come? " murmured Garnier, remembering again of a sudden the existence of Toto and his long absence.

"He is coming," he murmured, holding her hand; "he will be here in a little while. Oh, my dear little Célestin, what can I give you—what can I do for you?"

He saw the bunch of grapes, and plucked one off and held it to her lips. She sucked it feebly, and then cast her eyes up to heaven in the old familiar way, an action that tore Garnier's heart as if a knife had ripped it up. Then she seemed to forget Toto, for she lay still, and the man beside her prayed God to send him quickly, for nothing could be more frightful than her reiterated request for this man who had gone away.

He did not feel jealous; it was all one now. She wanted Toto. It was as if she had wanted water to drink; he would not have felt jealous of the water, so why should he feel jealous of Toto? He would have given his whole prospects in life for the return of the Prince.

As if in answer to his prayer came the sounds of footsteps in the atelier, and Dodor moved restlessly in his cage as the door was cautiously opened. It was a priest whom the deaf concierge had sent for after inquiring of Dr. Fénélon the state of his patient.

He was an elderly man with a large stomach and a kind, sweet face. Garnier glanced at him, and threw up his eyes, as if to say " No use," but he felt glad of the presence of the holy man.

The priest took a chair on the opposite side of the bed, as if to rest his stomach for a moment, and breathed hard and pursed out his lips; then he knelt by the chair to pray. Garnier, kneeling by his side of the bed, was as still as the effigy of the Lord Jesus which hung above. And so the time went on, Célestin rousing herself occasionally to call for Toto, and relapsing into stupor. Once she cast her eyes at the bird moping in its cage, and moved her lips at it, as if trying to tell it of her trouble.

It was now late in the afternoon. To Garnier it seemed a very long time since, stopping near the Panthéon, he had bought the grapes for his little Célestin, and brought them so joyously to the atelier. His hearing, strained to the utmost for the footsteps of Toto, was rewarded by all sorts of futile sounds, far away and near.

At five Dr. Fénélon looked in again, and found his patient unconscious. He shook his head and vanished, for Garnier did not attempt to detain him; he had lost all faith in doctors.

"But who is this Désiré she has been calling for?" whispered the good priest, leaning towards Garnier. "Could we not send for him?"

Garnier shook his head. He had gone out with Gaillard—where he could not tell.

Towards six, Célestin, still unconscious, gave a little shiver, as if at the coldness of her lover, and Dodor in the cage fluttered his wings as if in fear.

The priest, who had been standing patiently, fell upon his knees, and prayed with fervor for the passing soul.

.   .   .   .   .

Struve told me most of this story as we sat one day before a café on the boulevards.

"That is the man," he said, indicating a good-looking young fellow on a coal-black horse, who was riding by, accompanied by a girl with auburn hair, mounted on a magnificent gray; "that is Toto."

" But the girl? "

" His wife, the Princesse; she was Helen Powers."

" But surely—is she married to him? "

" Very much so. He confessed all his sins, and she gave him absolution. No woman, you see, can withstand a confession of folly; you see, it is a far more genuine thing than a confession of love— with ordinary men."

" You do not think Toto an ordinary man? "

" I have never thought of him as a man. Come, it is five o'clock; I am tired of sitting still."

" A moment. Where has old De Nani gone to? "

" He is living at Monte Carlo. He lost a hundred thousand francs there, and they have pensioned him; they give him sixty francs a week, I believe."

" Pelisson did not prosecute him? "

" Oh, no! all that did *Pantin* a lot of good."

" If I had been Toto, I would have made him fight."

" Thank goodness we were saved from that!   A duel between Toto and De Nani was the only thing wanted to cap the business and kill everyone outright."

" Kill them? "

" With laughter."

" And about Garnier? "

" Ah, Garnier—he only wanted one thing before he met Célestin."

" What was that? "

" Célestin—she has made him.   Célestin is not dead; she will never die so long as men have eyes and Garnier's pictures exist.   She might have lived with Toto and produced little Totos; she lives instead with Garnier, and through him will live forever."

" A moment.   What of Gaillard? "

" He has grown very fat.   You know, Toto shook him off when he married, Pelisson forsook him, De Brie gave him the cold shoulder; and what did he do?   He sat down and wrote ' Poum-

Poum,' and turned all the minor poets into ridi-
cule, and sold a hundred thousand copies in a
month, and ' slew art,' to use his own expression,
because it tried to slay him. He is making eighty
thousand francs a year, if he is making a sou. I am
glad of it; he is not a bad sort—Gaillard."

THE END.

January, 1899

HENRY HOLT & CO.'S RECENT BOOKS

The Publishers' list of GENERAL LITERATURE, *with portraits of Mrs. Voynich, Paul L. Ford, Anthony Hope, Jerome K. Jerome, and eighteen others, or their Educational Catalogue, free on application to 29 W. 23d St., New York.*

LAVIGNAC'S MUSIC AND MUSICIANS

Edited for America by H. E. KREHBIEL and translated by WILLIAM MARCHANT. With 94 illustrations and 510 examples in musical notation. 12mo.

A brilliant, sympathetic, and authoritative work covering musical sound, the voice, musical instruments, construction aesthetics, and the history of music.

BEERS' ENGLISH ROMANTICISM—XVIII CENTURY

Gilt top. 12mo. $2.00.

This is Professor Beers' most important work. Its chapters are : The Subject Defined, The Augustans, The Spenserians, The Landscape Poets, The Miltonic Group, The School of Warton, The Gothic Revival, Percy and the Ballads, Ossian, Thomas Chatterton, and The German Tributary. The author's style is admirably simple and clear, and has an undercurrent of humor. The sympathy and skill in character-drawing so notable in his *Suburban Pastoral* stories (75 cents) here serve to furnish vital and distinct portraits of the various romancers.

WALKER'S DISCUSSIONS IN EDUCATION

By the late FRANCIS A. WALKER, President of the Massachusetts Institute of Technology. Edited by JAMES P. MUNROE. 8vo. $3.00, *net, special.*

The author had hoped himself to collect these papers in a volume. They are grouped under *Technological Education, Manual Education, The Teaching of Arithmetic* and *College Problems* (including *College Athletics*). A *Valedictory* appropriately closes the book.

ADAMS' SCIENCE OF FINANCE

By HENRY C. ADAMS, Professor in the University of Michigan. *American Science Series. Advanced Course.* 8vo. $3.50, *net.*

The Review of Reviews : "The first American text-book of the science of public expenditures and public revenues . . . thoroughly systematic . . . apparently leaves no important topic related to the main subject untouched . . . luminous and suggestive."

JENKS' LAW AND POLITICS IN THE MIDDLE AGES   With a synoptic table of sources. 8vo. $2.75, *net.*

Harvard Law Review : "A valuable contribution to legal history. . . . A book of great merit, which displays wide learning."

HISTORIES OF LITERATURE

ENGLISH LITERATURE

Pancoast's Introduction to English Literature
With chronological tables, reading-lists, etc. 556 pp. 16mo. $1.25, net. (*Circular free.*)
"The style is interesting, the conception broad and clear, the biographical details nicely subordinated to matters more important."—*The Nation.*

Taine's English Literature
Library edition, 2 vols. 12mo. $5.00.
Four-volume edition, with 28 portraits. 12mo. $7.50.
Class-room edition. *Abridged by John Fiske.* 502 pp. 12mo. $1.40, net.

AMERICAN LITERATURE

Pancoast's Introduction to American Literature
With 13 portraits, chronological tables, and reading-lists. xiii + 393 pp. 16mo. $1.00, net.
"Quite the best brief manual of its subject that we know. . . . National traits are well brought out without neglecting organic connections with the mother country. Forces and movements are as well handled as personalities, the influence of writers hardly less than their individuality."—*The Nation.*

GERMAN LITERATURE

Francke's Social Forces in German Literature
577 pp. 8vo. $2.00, net.
A critical, philosophical, and historical account of German literature that is "destined to be a standard work for both professional and general uses" (*Dial*), and that has been translated in Germany. It begins with the sagas of the fifth century and ends with Hauptmann's "Hannele" (1894) (*Circular free.*)

Gostwick and Harrison's German Literature (380-1870)
xii + 588 pp. 12mo. $2.00, net.
Chiefly descriptive and biographical, with extracts in translation.

FRENCH LITERATURE

Fortier's Histoire de la Littérature Française
362 pp. 16mo. $1.00, net.
A compact and very readable account of French literature to our own day, written in French.

ITALIAN LITERATURE

Symonds' Italian Literature
With a portrait of the author. xv + 561 and x + 642 pp. 2 vols. 12mo. $4.00.
These two volumes constitute Part IV of the famous *History of the Renaissance in Italy*, by John Addington Symonds. They are complete in themselves.

GREEK LITERATURE

Perry's Greek Literature
Richly illustrated. xv + 877 pp. 8vo. $4.00.
A clear and sympathetic account, with sketches of representative works, including copious extracts in translation.

Postage on NET books, 8 per cent additional.

HENRY HOLT & CO., 29 W. 23d Street New York

LUCAS' A BOOK OF VERSES FOR CHILDREN

Over 200 poems, representing some 80 authors. Compiled by EDWARD VERRALL LUCAS. With title-page and cover-lining pictures in color by F. D. BEDFORD, two other illustrations, and white cloth cover in three colors and gilt. *Revised edition.* 12mo. $2.00.

Prof. Edward Everett Hale, Jr.: "David Copperfield remembered learning to walk, and Pierre Loti remembers the first time he jumped, I think. My earliest recollections are of being sung to sleep by my father, who used to sing for that purpose 'The British Grenadiers' and other old time songs. At about the same period it must have been that my mother introduced me to 'Meddlesome Mattie' and 'George and the Chimney-sweep.' It was, therefore, with a rush of recollection that on opening 'A Book of Verses for Children' compiled by Edward Verrall Lucas I discovered not only these three classics but many another lovely thing by Ann and Jane Taylor, Elizabeth Turner, and others, as well as more modern poems by Stevenson and Lewis Carroll. 'Can it be,' thought I, 'that children nowadays will stand Ann and Jane Taylor?' An opportunity of experiment came very soon. I happened to have the book under my arm the next day as I stopped to see some friends. They were out, so I asked for the children and had afternoon tea with real tea-things in company with a large and very beautiful doll, and afterward skated about the hall on what had originally been toy freight-cars. At last I asked if poems would be acceptable. The proposal was received with favor, and I was soon seated on a large trunk with Miss Geraldine on one side and Mr. Bartlett on the other. I began with a safe one, 'The Walrus and the Carpenter,' but went on with the Taylorian 'Birds, Beasts, and Fishes.' This took very well. I tried another modern (not to push a good thing into the ground), and then went on with 'Tommy and his Sister Jane.' This also succeeded, so I continued with others and others. We were finally interrupted in our delightful occupation, but I regarded the experiment as successful. . . . I know of nothing better to say of this book than the strictly accurate and unvarnished account I have just given. For my own part I thought it one of the most delightful books I had seen for a long time.

Critic: "We know of no other anthology for children so complete and well arranged."

New York Tribune: "The book remains a good one; it contains so much that is charming, so much that is admirably in tune with the spirit of childhood. Moreover, the few colored decorations with which it is supplied are extremely artistic, and the cover is exceptionally attractive."

Churchman: "Beautiful in its gay cover, laid paper, and decorated title page. Mr. Edward Verrall Lucas has made the selections with nice discrimination and an intimate knowledge of children's needs and capacities. Many of the selections are classic, all are refined and excellent. The book is valuable as a household treasure."

Bookman: "A very satisfactory book for its purpose, and has in it much that is not only well adapted to please and interest a rational child, but that is good, sound literature also."

Poet Lore: "A child could scarcely get a choicer range of verse to roll over in his mind, or be coaxed to it by a prettier volume . . . A book to take note of against Christmas and all the birthday gift times of the whole year round."

HENRY HOLT & CO.   29 West 28d Street
New York

(3)

Lightning Source UK Ltd.
Milton Keynes UK
UKHW012154120119

335365UK00007BB/503/P